TO AVOID FAINTING

KEEP REPEATING:

IT'S ONLY A MAGAZINE

. . . ONLY A MAGAZINE

. . . ONLY A MAGAZINE

. . . ONLY A MAGAZINE

. . . ONLY A MAGAZINE

PERPETUAL MOTION MACHINE PUBLISHING
Cibolo, Texas
www.DarkMoonDigest.com

Dark Moon Digest—Issue Forty-Four

PMMP
dark moon

www.darkmoondigest.com
www.patreon.com/pmmppublishing
www.pmmpnews.com
darkmoonhorror@gmail.com

ARTWORK CREDITS

Cover and Table of Contents Artwork by Allen Koszowski
Interior Artwork by Lori Michelle

DARK MOON DIGEST

ISSUE #44

FICTION

NON-FICTION

Publishers

Max Booth III & Lori Michelle

Editor-in-Chief

Lori Michelle

Managing Editor

Max Booth III

Columnists

George Daniel Lea

Jay Wilburn

Founder & Publisher Emeritus

Stan Swanson

DARK MOON DIGEST is published four times a year (January, April, July, and October) by Perpetual Motion Machine Publishing in print format as well as an e-magazine version.

All correspondence should be addressed (via e-mail) to the Editor-in-Chief at *DarkMoonHorror@gmail.com*.

Cost per issue for **Dark Moon Digest** is $7.95 for the print edition and $2.99 for the e-publication version which are available in Kindle and Nook formats.

Print editions are available from the publisher at **PerpetualPublishing.com** as well as major online bookstores including Amazon, Barnes & Noble, and many other book dealers. Bulk orders are available through the publisher.

Story submission must be made via Submittable at **https://darkmoon digest.submittable.com/submit** or following the links on our website **www.PerpetualPublishing.com** or blog, **www.DarkMoonDigest.com**. Make sure you follow the submission guidelines which can be found on Submittable. Failure to do so could result in your submission being rejected for consideration.

All submissions are read by a minimum of 3 editors, so please allow 90 to 120 days after submitting for response. We encourage simultaneous submissions as we understand the perspective from the writer's side. However, please withdraw your submission if your work is accepted elsewhere. Any submission questions can be directed to the Editor-in-Chief at *DarkMoonHorror@gmail.com*.

THANK YOU TO OUR SUPPORTERS ON PATREON.

A.J Spencer, Adam Rains, Adrian Shotbolt, Alex Ebenstein, Allison Henry-Plotts, Amanda Niehaus-Hard, Andrew Shaffer, Antony Klancar, Austin Martin, Ben Walker, Betty Rocksteady, Beverly, Bill Morrow, Bob, Bob Pottle, Brandon Petry, Brett Reistroffer, Brian Asman, Brian K Hauser, Charlotte Platt, Chas Phx, Chris Baumgartner, Christina Booth, Cindy Gunnin, Claudia J Parker, Cockroach Conservatory, Crystal Lake Publishing, Cut, Dai Baddley, Dan Howarth, Daniel Scamell, Dave, David Demchuk, David Perlmutter, David Thirteen, DeerNoises, Drew Purcell, Emma Williamson, Erin Murphy-Jay, Eve Harms, Franklin Charles Murdock, Gengar, George Daniel Lea, Gerardo Pelayo, Grant Longstaff, Gregory A. Martin, Ian Muller, Ingrid Taylor, Jack Smiles, James (Tony) Evans, Jampersand, Jason Kawa, Jay Wilburn, Jennifer Dury, Jennifer McCarthy, Jessica Leonard, Jessica McHugh, John Foster, John Rockwell, Jose Triana, Joseph Zablocki, Julie Cyburt, Karla K Ridpath, Keith Burton, Kev Harrison, Kevin Lovecraft, Kit Michael-Ryan, Lee Widener, Lloyd Hanneman, Lou Columbus, Mark Jones, Matt Gamble, Matt Neil Hill, Matthew Booth, Matthew Brandenburg, Matthew Henshaw, Melodie Ladner, Michael Louis Dixon, Michael O'Brien, Miguel_myers, Myrmidon, Nichole Neely, Nick Petrou, Night Worms, Nikolas P. Robinson, Patrick Tumblety, Paul Ramage, PirateFrequencies, Rachel Cassidy, Randall Lee Lovejoy, Rebecca , Richard Gerlach, Richard Martin, Richard Staving, Rob Bose, Rob Gibbs, Robert S. Wilson, Roger Venable, S. Kay Nash, Scott Beggs, Shelby MacLeod, Sheri White, Sherry Solorio, Stephen Helmig, Steve Ringman, Steven Campbell, Steven Schlozman, Stewie , Theresa Gillmore, This Is Horror, Thomas Joyce, Tim, Todd Keisling, Traci Kenworth, Tyler Cooper, Vincenzo Bilof, Webberly Rattenkraft, Will Griskevich, William Hull, Wookie PornHub in Alderaan Places, and Zachary Ashford

Want your name added to this page and saved for eternity? Head on over to www.patreon.com/pmmpublishing and become a patron.

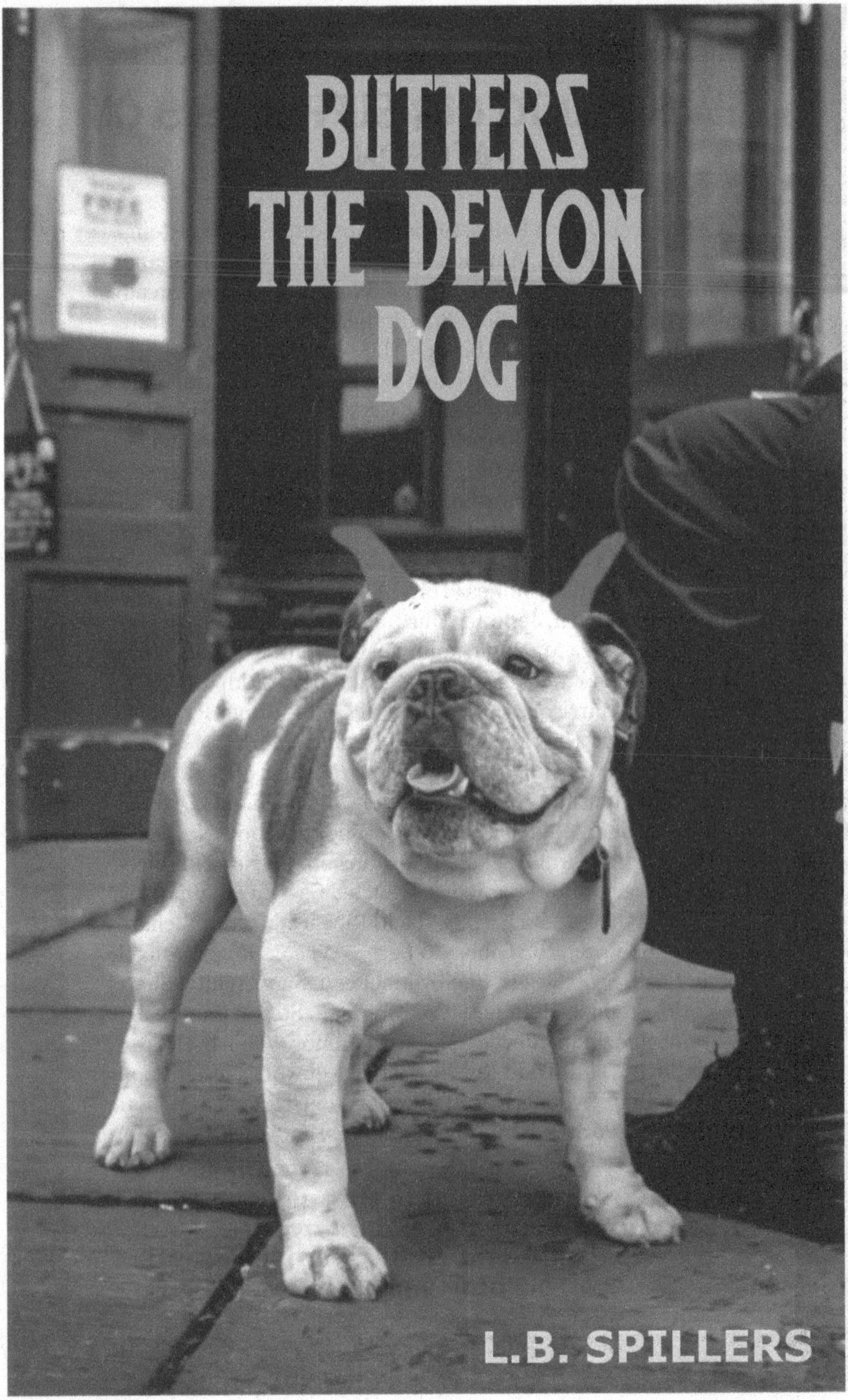
BUTTERS
THE DEMON
DOG
L.B. SPILLERS

THE FIRST TIME I suspected my English bulldog wasn't normal was on a breezy spring day. The nice weather meant that instead of lazing around inside, buffeting us with his astounding farts, Butters was outside manifesting his alter ego, Professor Chaos.

A mewing stuffed cat got him wound up. The fact that I was holding the toy and teasing him mercilessly with it was, of course, no fault of mine. Butters was snarling, and I was getting nipped occasionally. I didn't get mad. If you're going to play rough with a dog, you're going to get a little banged up. When things started to get out of hand, I gently dominated him in good Dog Whisperer style. I held him down on his side until he relaxed.

My mistake was to rub it in.

Before releasing him I leaned in close to stare in his eyes and yelled "Gamma, you turd-mongering bastard! You're not alpha, not beta, but gamma!" I guess I was a little mad after all.

An hour later he took a crap in the form of a lower-case alpha. Since it's just a long turd with a loop in it, I took it as a humorous coincidence. In retrospect, everything looks more ominous. I was the guy in the horror movie who couldn't see the obvious signs. In my defense, I thought I was living a dramedy.

***

Decoding my dog's behavior was low on my list of priorities. I had a pile of first-world problems: annoying boss, slacker co-workers, and the burgeoning realization that I had already peaked. Even with all that, I tended to brood on my neighbors. It's about proximity. You get up and go to sleep knowing that scant yards away a clan of slack-jawed, trashy idiots were gleefully proving Darwin wrong. These offensive morons bred like rabbits, and showed no signs of being culled from the herd. In fact, the youngest in my least favorite neighbor's house was a seventeen-year-old miscreant who had already passed on his seed. His father recounted the story to me with false lament and a telling glint in his eye which said "my boy is an unstoppable force of nature" as if knocking up some high-school girl proved he had raised a thoroughbred.

Who cares, right? I mean the world is full of offensive asses. How near or far their ass-clownery occurs is hardly relevant. It's like cursing the weather. You'll go crazy if you let it bother you.

Normally I can get behind that sentiment. But this neighbor had a jacked-up, silver pickup truck that rode a good two feet off the ground with enormous tires and a V-8 that you could hear idling a mile away. Since I lived only fifty yards away, it was hard to ignore. As far as my girlfriend Doris and I have been able to tell, the monstrous nature of his truck has no actual utility in his daily routine, but we hear it every morning and evening. If we're home, we hear it coming and going throughout the day. Doris says the guy is an insecure alpha-male wannabee. She calls it the penis truck. Its size and noise announce just how big his phallus isn't.

One penis truck is bad enough, but they run in packs. There are days when a second and even a third one will add its voice to the automotive auto-eroticism. Each has an after-market exhaust system that ekes out another few horsepower by not actually muffling the exhaust. So when the throaty trucks are in conference, nose to tail allowing their drivers to chat, the thunderous idling noise of the things rattles the panes of glass in my front storm door.

These thoughts were distracting me one day while I was walking Butters. It took several shouts to bring me back to the present so I could witness the second clue that Butters was more than your average dog.

I hadn't noticed that a neighbor had been yelling at me to stop, over and over. She was struggling to control her own dog, so what little of my brain that was listening thought she was yelling at her unruly mastiff. I kept going down the sidewalk towards her house until she said "Sir, halt!" in a tone that indicated that 'sir' was a stand-in for something far more vulgar. More bemused than anything, I complied.

Butters dutifully sat on his haunches next to me. Not the typical bulldog color, he is what the AKC calls 'fawn brindle'—a beautiful brown with vertical tiger-like stripes and white accents. He's as well behaved as he is good looking. The little under-bite makes him impossibly cute.

"I don't think she respects your authoritah, Butters," I said to him. "She's messing up your walk, and addressing your human quite rudely."

I often talked to Butters like an adult. His face is so expressive that I think I see meaningful reactions in it. This time, Butters got one of those contemplative looks on his face, wise and dispassionate with just a hint of sadness. It looked nothing less than sentient. He replied with a rare, quiet woof.

Immediately the noise from my neighbor changed. Her mastiff,

Pookie, jerked on her leash hard enough to shut her owner up and pull her off balance. As the lady did a face plant on her lawn, Pookie ran out of the open gate and sprinted towards Butters and me.

Butters didn't flinch as the massive dog bore down on us. I didn't either. I'm a dog guy. Dogs like me, and I like dogs. Pookie sensed all this and came to a skittering halt in front of us, clearly overjoyed to meet us. I smiled at her and patted her head while murmuring doggie praise.

Pookie lowered herself to the ground before Butters, her tail wagging too fast to see. Meanwhile her bitchy owner was cursing me as she raised her fleshy frame off the ground. Somehow her inability to control her dog or close her gate was my fault.

The mastiff and Butters engaged in delicate nasal communion until the mastiff's owner was dumb enough to yell "You keep your damn mutt away from her." Maybe she didn't see how Pookie had clearly joined our pack. Maybe she didn't see Butters' magnificent pedigree. The absurdity of it made me laugh.

Butters seemed less amused at the slight to his lineage. His ears twitched. Those large, empathetic, watery eyes of his narrowed. An exasperated little groan came out of him, the kind he uses with us when he doesn't get his way. Hearing that, Pookie sprinted back to her yard, and set on her ill-mannered owner.

"Proper," I said, nodding at Butters. His corkscrew tail responded with a few excited cycles.

We lazily resumed our stroll down the sidewalk, enjoying the show. Pookie ran looping patterns in her yard, body-slamming her owner every time she regained her feet. When we reached her gate, Butters stared the owner in the eyes while Pookie urinated on her prone form.

You have to see it from my point of view. This wasn't my dog wielding arcane powers. This was a stupid owner unable to compete with the sense of community our little mobile pack offered Pookie. There was no blood or serious injury, just an ill-tempered woman receiving her comeuppance.

It was funny to me. I live in a dramedy. Comic relief is half the reason to own a dog.

***

I was completely disillusioned a month later. When I stepped inside my front door, I immediately knew something was off. Growling came from the back yard, a soft chorus in curious pitches and cadences. I had to strain to hear it. About three seconds after cocking my ear, it cut off. Then there was a symphony of muffled sounds: thuds, tapping, rustling, skittering, and the distinctive rattle of the chain link fence.

When I walked out back, Butters was sitting in the middle of the yard facing the door. His ears were up. Rather than running to me as he usually would, he continued to sit for a few seconds giving me a knowing, happy look. He waited while I scanned the yard looking for the source of the noises.

Again, in retrospect, it was creepy. It's like he didn't want to interrupt me reassuring myself that there was nothing going on. His canine Jedi-mind-trick complete, he sprinted over to me with his little corkscrew tail thrumming at a gleeful frequency. Happy dogs are very reassuring, and distracting. So when I saw Butters do his oh-my-god-you're-home shtick, I put everything else out of my mind. The delay was odd, but the emotion was so genuine I just chalked it up to bulldog oddness. Butters was inscrutable.

That evening my suspicions resurfaced. I didn't say anything to Doris because she would worry herself to distraction. If put to the test, I think she would choose me over him, but I'd rather not see it played out.

I logged onto our home security website and pulled up the back yard video record. Minutes before I arrived home, the back yard was filled with twenty neighborhood dogs respectfully arrayed before Butters. I almost choked on my beer.

My mind was already working hard to avoid the truth. I rationalized that a bunch of dogs hanging out in my yard acknowledging Butters as alpha was something to be proud of. That weak explanation held only a few seconds. When I saw their reactions to me coming home, I shivered. They held formation while Butters turned briefly to look in the direction of the house. Then, as a synchronized group, all the dogs scattered like a band of ninjas melting into the background.

My back yard is completely fenced, so there were scenes of incredible poochie parkour as many of the dogs performed acrobatic bounds which propelled them over the low fence making use of the garbage cans and the lawn furniture. The smallest dogs slipped through gaps in the three gates. The less nimble of the medium-sized dogs were helped by a Rottweiler who served as a step. He stood next to the fence, and they bounded onto his back and over the top with fearless élan. The Rottweiler then did something I'd never seen a dog do. His hundred pounds wouldn't easily take the three-foot barrier in one leap, so in mid-jump he used his front paws to give his bulk the boost it needed to clear the fence.

When I saw the vacant look on my face in the video, I was chilled. I was not alpha. Butters was handling me. But to what end?

***

I hadn't understood it, but Butters had been slowly acclimating me to his arcane nature. That time I got home and heard the tail end of his canine conclave, he had purposefully delayed dismissing the group so I would catch a piece of it. No doubt, he heard my car pull up, the car door close, and my key ring jangling at the front step. Butters had plenty of time to clear the yard with me none the wiser.

That gentle indoctrination took a hard turn late one night. I got up at 2am to let him out to pee. Rather than finding him curled up on his bed with his tongue hanging comically out of his mouth, he was instead awake and alert, waiting for me.

It was a cool, moonless spring night. He dutifully loped off to one side of the yard to do his business—both barrels that evening. Then, instead of trotting back to me eager to return to sleep, he crossed to the other side of the yard where the back light didn't reach.

Curious, I shuffled over there in my flip-flops and was stunned to see three other dogs waiting there. A beautiful Siberian Husky was holding down my neighbor's Siamese cat lightly with a paw. The agile Rottweiler was supervising, and a Chihuahua was standing guard near the cat's head. Anytime the terrified cat so much as twitched, the Chihuahua swatted it cruelly with its sharp little claws. Pound for pound, Chihuahuas are one of the most fearsome dogs you'll ever meet.

The cat looked at me, pleading with its eyes. The dogs looked only at Butters. Without so much as a chuff out of any of them, Butters reared lightly onto his back legs. His narrow bulldog waist gave him astounding balance.

Butters' left paw scratched at the air. The muscles in his ground legs flexed, exerting a tremendous force in the effort. Blue fire trailed his paw as it moved. Gesturing slowly in this way, it took him several seconds to trace a flaming glyph in the air. Resembling Indian script, it rippled like it was drawn on an invisible fabric fluttering in the breeze.

On some silent cue, the three other dogs bounded away, and the glyph sheet wrapped around the cat just as it regained its feet. The cat became a brilliant flash of blue light that streaked to the corners of the property, bathing the yard in a diffuse haze.

When I got over my shock, I realized the three neighborhood dogs were gone. Butters was sitting, watching me intently. Flecks of blue fire danced in his eyes. I stepped to where the cat had been immolated and pawed at the ground with my flip-flop. I kept at it overlong, drawing reassurance from the pushback of the Earth. After seeing Butters carve the air into something which swallowed up a cat, I enjoyed the reassurance that reality was where I left it.

I don't know if it was another canine Jedi-mind-trick, but when I looked back at Butters, I had this sense that despite his power, he was still my dog, my impossibly cute, good dog.

"You know I hate cats, buddy," I said. "Good riddance to that Siamese prick. But don't let Doris see anything like that. She doesn't understand how evil cats are."

Butters tilted his head in the classic confused-dog style. It was my turn to be nonchalant. I ignored him and headed back inside. After a second, he followed at my heels.

***

I had a demon dog. After witnessing a blood sacrifice, there wasn't room for misinterpretation, even in the dumbest horror movie. The question was: should I care? Let's face it, Butters had good judgment. Pookie's owner needed an adjustment, and the fewer Siamese cats in this world the better.

Butters didn't demand better treatment. He never turned on me or addressed me in some satanic voice. As far as I could tell, he was the same stubborn, lovable, playful pain in the ass he always was. I decided to roll with it, mostly because I couldn't bear the thought of telling Doris about it.

Once the truth was out, the gifts started showing up. Cans of luxury dog food, and bags of high-end kibble would appear on our lawn. Dog toys, some still in their packaging would show up on our doorstep. Doris thought it was marvelous. The other dogs loved Butters so much that they brought him stuff. In her mind it made sense. I never told her the truth. It was partly out of fear of her reaction, and partly out of respect for Butters. No doubt he could have arranged a demonstration for her if he thought it was needed. There was a precarious equilibrium to the situation that I couldn't imagine improving with an intervention.

We had reached an understanding, he and I. I was alpha in my world, and he in his. His growing material wealth was fine with me. When Doris wasn't around, I would open the pantry door and ask him what his pleasure was. He would survey his minion's offerings and paw at his preference. High-quality meat on a bed of overpriced, soft kibble was his usual favorite.

I was content, but not as vigilant as I should have been. One day while Doris was at the store I made a horrible mistake. When she wasn't around, I could talk to Butters like the sentient being he was. He never answered with more than a look, but it was a kind of man-dog bonding that we engaged in when we had privacy.

Seated in front of the TV watching Dr. Pohl, we were interrupted by the penis truck. Butters gave me a questioning look when I reached for the remote to turn the sound up. Four beers into the evening, it just slipped out.

"That truck needs to go, Butters," I said slouching back onto the leather couch. Lying next to me, Butters lifted his head. Knowing that he was paying attention, I should have stopped, but I just let it fly.

"That guy needs to learn some respect, and his son needs to be neutered so that his over-chlorinated gene pool doesn't leak any further into the population."

Butters huffed what I took to be a laugh. I felt clever that my use of the word 'neutered' got a chuckle out of him. It was man-doggie bonding at its best.

A week later, Butters scrabbled at the front door. That was unusual because we generally didn't let him out front where there was no fence. Curious, I went with him. He sat on his haunches facing my neighbor's house. Seconds later we heard the approach of the penis truck.

Knowing Butters as I did, him calmly sitting, waiting with purpose like that, gave me a chill. When I saw the dog turd in my neighbor's usual parking spot softly glowing blue I silently mouthed an "Oh Shit."

The penis truck rolled up with my neighbor and his son in it, oblivious to the presence of the arcane shit pile underneath. The man popped the hood, and went to the front of the truck. I was impressed to see that there was a little platform bolted underneath which he rotated out so he could stand on it and work on his engine.

The guy futzed with something and yelled for his son to give it some gas. A flash of blue light burst from the engine. Startled, he pulled his head out of the compartment. Immediately yellow flames and an explosion followed, engulfing the father's torso. Simultaneously, the truck cab was filled with dust.

I called 911 before running over to help. Butters stayed sitting where he was. I used my neighbor's hose to put out the fire and ease the pain of his burns. Some neighborhood first responder was on the scene in less than two minutes. By the time I had water on the fire, he was working on getting the son out.

Distant sirens approached. I looked at Butters across the street. Despite all the noise and smell, he sat still and serene on our lawn, like some bulldog Buddha.

The next day Doris got a report from her network of neighborhood ladies. The father suffered second-degree burns on a third of his torso. The debris propelled into the cabin had destroyed his son's genitals, just like I had told Butters was needed. Unfortunately, it also ripped a femoral artery. The boy was dead. Butters killed that boy because of what I said.

When Doris finished her report, I stared at Butters, trying to reconcile the perfect, playful bastard I raised with the murdering demon he'd become. He came over and nuzzled my leg before looking up at me with a question in his big, innocent eyes.

"You're a good boy, Butters," I said, petting his head.

His corkscrew tail wiggled in appreciation.

A refugee from software development, L. B. Spillers lives in Pueblo, Colorado with his girlfriend and two dogs, Butters and Dizzy (Butters is a sweetheart in real life). He splits his time between renovating his century-old house and writing. You can see what he's up to by visiting LBSpillers.com.

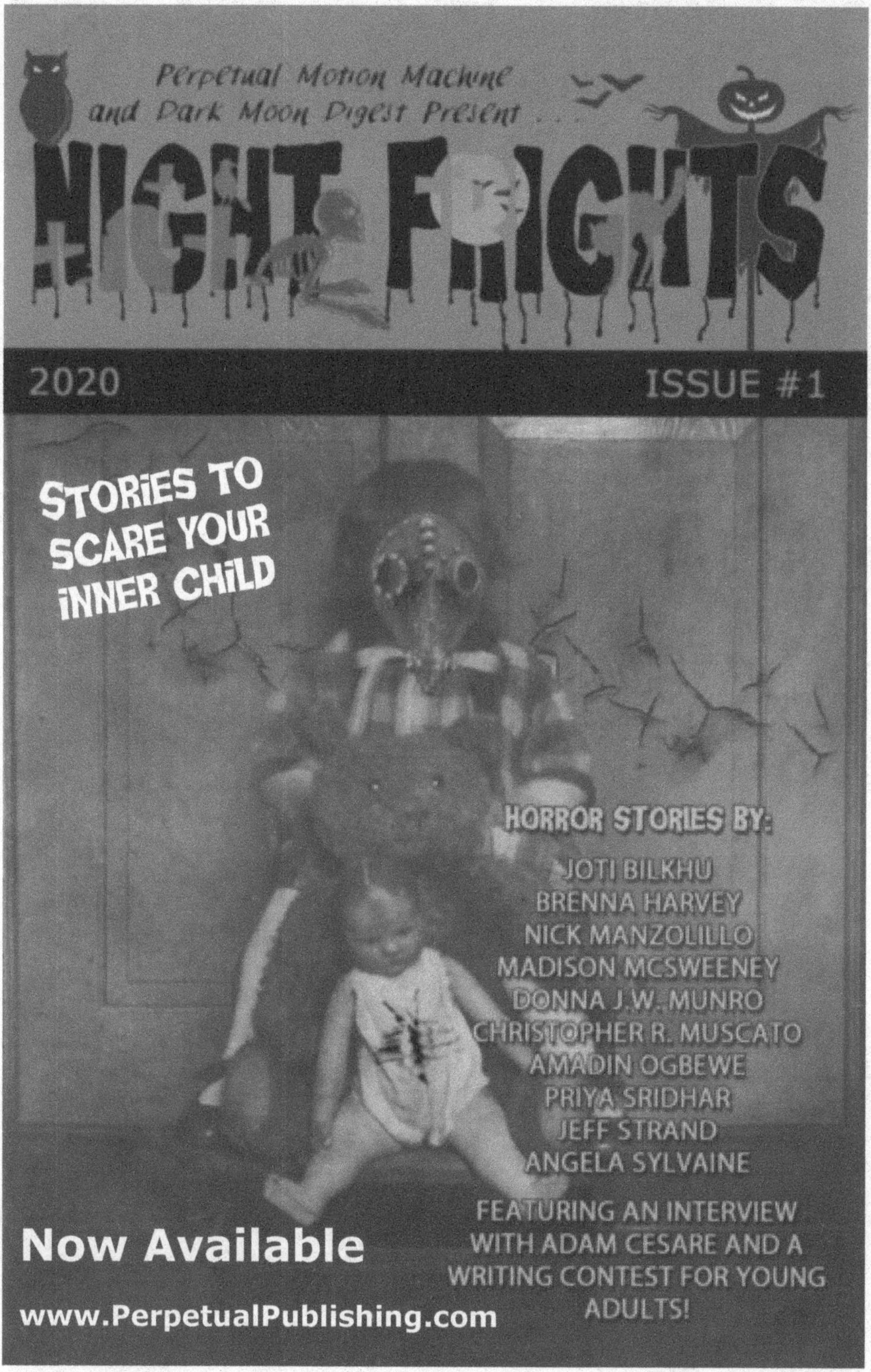
Perpetual Motion Machine
and Dark Moon Digest Present . . .
NIGHT FRIGHTS
2020
ISSUE #1
STORIES TO SCARE YOUR INNER CHILD
HORROR STORIES BY:
JOTI BILKHU
BRENNA HARVEY
NICK MANZOLILLO
MADISON MCSWEENEY
DONNA J.W. MUNRO
CHRISTOPHER R. MUSCATO
AMADIN OGBEWE
PRIYA SRIDHAR
JEFF STRAND
ANGELA SYLVAINE
FEATURING AN INTERVIEW WITH ADAM CESARE AND A WRITING CONTEST FOR YOUNG ADULTS!
Now Available
www.PerpetualPublishing.com

BROTHER TUBRO

DOMINICK CANCILLA

ADI SAT AT the kitchen table with *Mighty Trucks* open in front of him. His dead twin looked over his shoulder, standing because giving Tubro a chair would be asking for trouble.

Tubro was a little shorter and a lot thinner than Adi, and his head had a sort of dent on one side, like it was a pillow in the morning. The eye by the dent always stared, and the hair was patchy on that side, too. His skin was pale, probably from being dead, and nobody but Adi could see him.

Adi couldn't remember meeting or naming Tubro; the two of them had been inseparable since forever.

"This is a wheel loader," Adi said, pointing at the picture. "This is a tire. This is the bucket. This is the lift arm. This is the cab. This is Olivia, who drives the wheel loader." Adi looked from the book to Tubro and said, in a conspiratorial tone, "Olivia's just for the book. She isn't real."

"Tire?" Tubro asked, touching a dirty-nailed finger to the bottom of the cab.

"Close," Adi said. He touched the two visible tires in turn. "Tire, tire."

In the middle of her chores, Mom walked into the kitchen. "What're you doing, Sport?" she asked, opening the junk drawer to look for something or other.

"Reading my truck book," Adi said. He was the best reader in his class. Ms. Lannex said he was at a third-grade level. Because he was always reading, some of his classmates called him "bookshit," which Adi didn't even think was a word. He didn't mention this to Mom. Also, even though they were having a lesson, he didn't mention Tubro.

"That's nice," Mom said. She took the tape out of the drawer and looked at it.

"Honey," Dad called from the living room. "What's a seven-letter word for 'Argentinian city?'" He had been doing crosswords on his iPad since Adi got home from school an hour ago.

"Cordoba," Mom called back. Apparently giving up on the question of why she'd gotten the tape, she put it back in the drawer.

"Or Rosario," Tubro said. "Or Mendoza."

"Thank you," Dad called back.

"Welcome," Mom said.

"Dumb shits," added Tubro.

"Stop it," whispered Adi to his brother.

"What's that, Sport?" Mom asked.

"Nothing," Adi said. He needed a diversion. "I'm reading truck parts out loud."

Mom took his lunch box off the table beside Adi. "You've read that one a bunch of times, haven't you?" she asked, standing so Adi was the filling in a Mom-and-Tubro sandwich.

"Yes," Adi said. She knew he had a whole series of books on different types of vehicles because until he turned four he insisted that she read them to him over and over. It was weird that she had to ask, but Mom forgot things sometimes.

He took a dry Cheerio from the little bowl beside his book and ate it. Tubro took one, too. The first time Adi had gotten his own snack, he's gotten two bowls—one for him and one for Tubro. Mom had cried when she saw that, so he didn't do it again.

Mom took his lunch box to the counter. "Are you out of things to read?" she asked. "We can go to the library this weekend and get you some other books."

"Okay," Adi said. "I just feel like reading this one now, though." Adi and Tubro had been working on this book for two weeks. They did it in secret, just like they did lots of things in secret.

Tubro was as smart as Adi and he could read and remember things really well, but for some reason he couldn't see a word and a picture and match them up. It was something Adi had decided to work with him on using truck books, but so far they hadn't made much progress.

"What's this?" Mom asked. The lunch box was open in front of her and she had a folded paper in her hand. "Did you draw me a picture?"

"No," said Adi.

"Oh, shit," said Tubro. He used a lot of words that Adi couldn't use at home.

Mom unfolded the paper. "It's from Ms. Lannex," she said.

Adi hadn't known there was a note in his lunch box. Ms. Lannex must have put it there during recess. Now that he was a big kid, the teacher didn't go out with them to recess like when he was in kindergarten. She would have had a lot of time to put a note in there.

He wasn't sure what it was about, but it couldn't be anything good. When Ms. Lannex had a nice note or needed a Mom or Dad to sign something, she just gave it to him.

"I don't think that's for me," Adi said.

"It's *for* me," Mom said, her eyes moving over the paper. "It's *about* you."

"I didn't do anything," Adi said.

"What did you do?" Tubro asked. You can't lie to a twin.

"Honey," Mom called out.

"Hmm?" Dad called back.

"Can you come here for a second?"

"What is it?"

"Adi's teacher sent a note home from school."

"That's nice."

"No it's—can you please come here and see this?"

"I'll be done in a minute," Dad said.

"Fine," Mom said, largely to herself. Then, to Adi, "Come here so we can talk about this." She wasn't loud, but sounded stiff. It was her controlled-distress voice.

Adi got up from his chair and went to his mother, leaving his book, snack, and Tubro behind. She held the note for him to read. He did.

"Is this true?" Mom asked.

Adi read over the note again, hoping he'd missed something. "No." He knew where this was going and felt tears start to push into his eyes.

Mom knelt down so she was on his level. She took both of his hands in hers. "You know Daddy and I love you," she said.

Tubro made a scoffing noise, but Adi ignored him.

"We want what's best," she continued, "and we want you to be happy. But for that to happen, you have to trust us. Do you understand?"

Adi nodded. He felt like if he said even a word he might start crying. He didn't want to cry anymore today.

"Ms. Lannex says you had a problem at school today."

Adi nodded.

"Some of the kids were teasing you. Is that right?"

Adi nodded.

"Was it about Tubro?"

That did it. Adi overflowed with tears, a full-on dam burst.

Mom enveloped him in her arms. "It's okay. It's okay," she said.

His breath started to hitch and he could feel the pressure of blood in his face, like he was swelling up with humiliation. The note didn't say that two of the boys had hit him, and it didn't say they'd called him a baby and asked if he had tea parties. He didn't understand what that last part was, but he knew they meant it as an insult, and that was enough.

Remembering made him cry harder. Keeping secret details made him cry harder. Knowing he'd disobeyed made him cry harder.

Mom stroked Adi's hair, whispered in his ear that it was going to be okay.

After a while, Adi started calming down, finding control again. Mom had gotten a cloth napkin at some point and was wiping the damp from his face.

"That help?" Mom asked.

Still unsure about talking, Adi nodded. He took the napkin and wiped his nose.

"Were you going to keep to yourself?" Mom asked.

Adi nodded.

"Use your words," she said.

"Yes," Adi squeaked.

Mom, still down at his level, smiled. "I get it, Sport," she said. "Bullying is bad. Nobody likes to talk about it. But now do you see why you can't talk about Tubro at school?"

"Oh, for God's sake!" Dad called from the other room. "Seriously?"

"I've got this," Mom called back. "Do your puzzle."

"Asshole," Tubro added.

Mom took a deep breath. "I know you think Tubro is your special friend. Lots of children your age have special friends. I bet you don't hear them talking about them at school, though, do you?"

Adi shook his head.

"Words," Mom said.

"No," Adi said.

"Right. That's because those special friends are for at home, not for out in the world. They're for family ears only."

"But not Tubro," Adi said.

"No shit," said Tubro.

"Well, no," said Mom, "usually not Tubro. Tubro is a little different because—" Mom hesitated, and for a moment Adi thought she was going to cry herself, which would have been the worst thing of all. Then she pulled herself together and continued. "—because Tubro was my real baby."

"Who you mangled," Tubro said.

"Born right here in this house, just like you," Mom said.

"By parents too dumb to use a doctor."

"We wanted what was best for our babies, and hospitals aren't always the best. We had a midwife to help with the birth but when we found you were twins and that Mommy had some health problems, the midwife said we had to use a hospital and we couldn't do that."

"And fucked up the first baby."

"We loved you both so much."

"That you buried one in the back yard."

"But you can't talk about it, Sport," Mom said, finally letting herself cry. "You can't talk about it to anyone. It hurts Mommy to think about it. And if people found out, the police might take Mommy and Daddy away. You wouldn't want that, would you?"

"No!" Adi said. Then they were both crying and holding each other in the middle of the kitchen floor.

In the blur when he opened his eyes, Adi saw Tubro standing behind Mom.

"They don't really love you," Tubro said. "If you do something that might get them in trouble, they'll get rid of you, too."

"Stop it!" Adi yelled.

"What the hell?" Dad called from the other room.

"I'm sorry," Mom said. "I'm sorry. I didn't mean to lose control like that. I just love you so much. Even though I could only have him for a little while, I loved your brother, too. I really did. Not a day passes he isn't on my mind."

"What's going on here?" Dad asked, walking into the kitchen on heavy feet.

"We're just having a talk," Mom said.

Dad put a hand on Adi's shoulder and gently pulled him away from Mom. "You make Mom cry, young man?"

"You're a worthless sack of shit," Tubro said, looking at Dad.

"Nothing like that," Mom said.

"Well, I don't like it," Dad said.

"I'm going to put sleeping pills in your food," Tubro said.

"I'm sorry," Adi said.

"All right," Dad said. "That's enough of that."

"I'm going to stab you in your sleep until I'm tired," Tubro said. "Then you can see how *I* feel."

"Go play in your room," Dad said. He gave Adi a little swat on the behind. "Mom and I are going to have some grownup talk."

"Okay," Adi said. He wiped his eyes on his sleeve and kissed Mom on the cheek. Then he got his book and snack from the table and went to his room, Tubro following close behind.

Mom got up off the floor and took Dad's hand.

They stood in silence until they heard the click of Adi's bedroom door closing. Then Dad leaned into Mom and said quietly, "You okay?"

"I was just surprised," she said. She moved closer to hug him, then after they held each other for a moment, she whispered, "I think we'd better get a lock for the medicine cabinet."

"Amen to that," Dad said. Then they shared a kiss before he went back to his puzzle and she tried to find a better place in the kitchen to hide the knives.

Dominick Cancilla is the author of Tomorrow's Journal, *a novel in which family issues have global consequences. He has a spouse, a kid, and a sister, but no brothers with an objectively verifiable existence.*

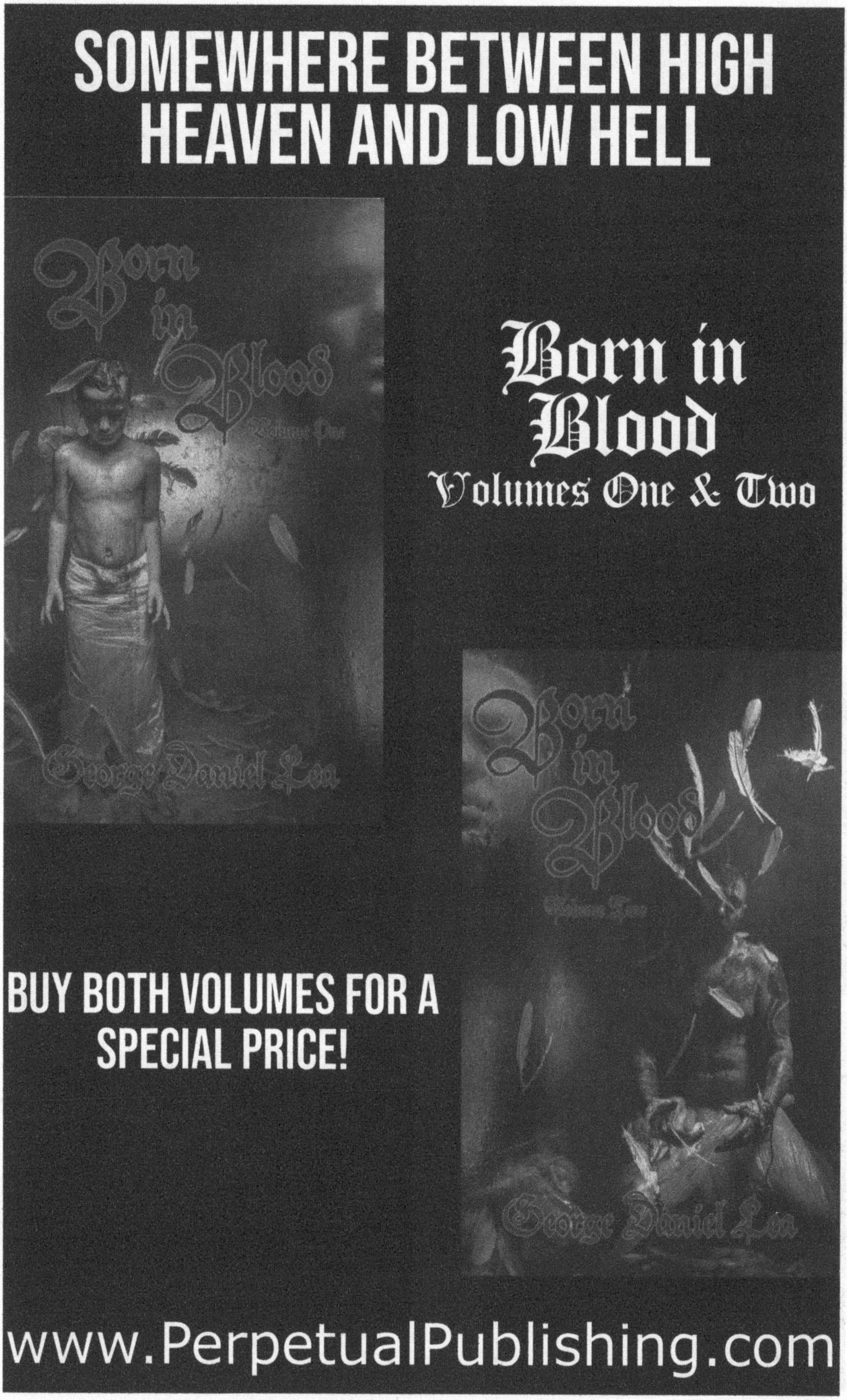
SOMEWHERE BETWEEN HIGH HEAVEN AND LOW HELL
Born in Blood
George Daniel Lea
Born in Blood
Volumes One & Two
Born in Blood
George Daniel Lea
BUY BOTH VOLUMES FOR A SPECIAL PRICE!
www.PerpetualPublishing.com

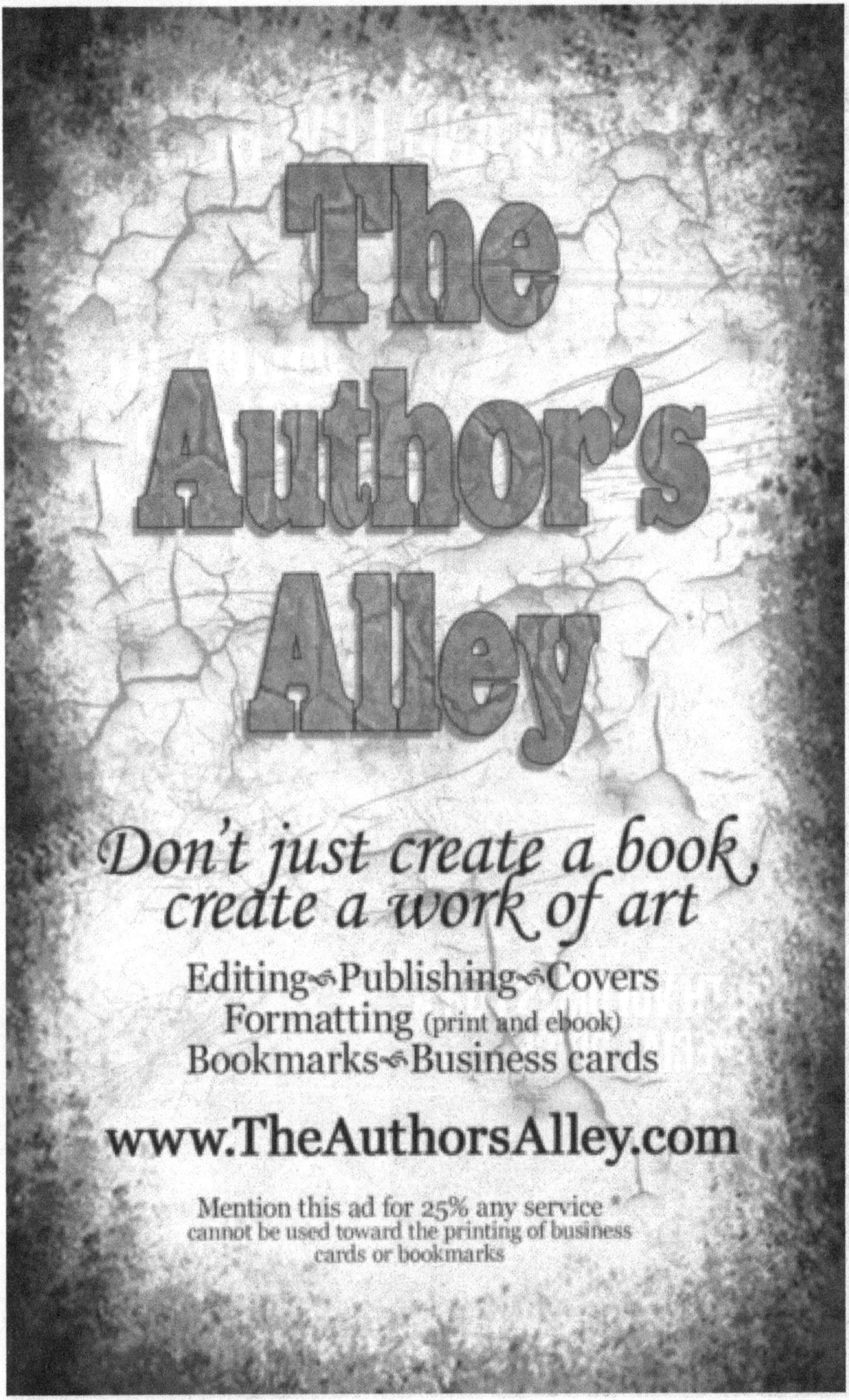
The Author's Alley
Don't just create a book, create a work of art
Editing Publishing Covers
Formatting (print and ebook)
Bookmarks Business cards
www.TheAuthorsAlley.com
Mention this ad for 25% any service *
cannot be used toward the printing of business cards or bookmarks

For Robby and his friends, an urban legend is the last thing on their minds when a boring Friday night presents a chance to download porn. But the short clip they watch turns out to be something far more graphic and disturbing, and in the coming days, they'll learn even the most outlandish urban legends possess a shred of truth…

SCANLINES

TODD KEISLING

**PERPETUAL MOTION
MACHINE PUBLISHING**

www.PerpetualPublishing.com

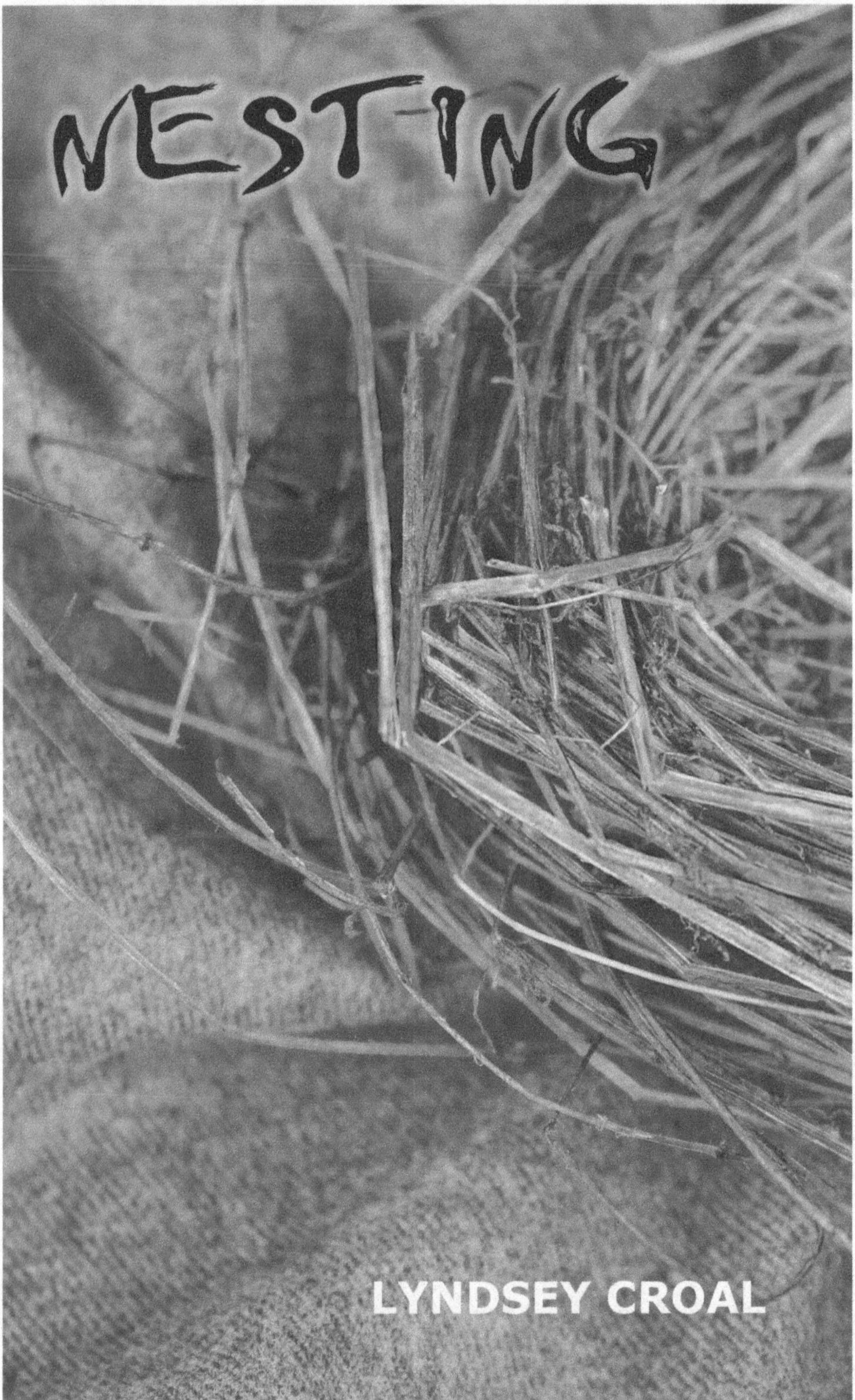
NESTING
LYNDSEY CROAL

HER JAW ACHES, *like claws are pulling at her teeth, as if searching for parts, removing them one by one until there's nothing left but a gaping maw, and there are stones in her throat so that she can't breathe, then something tickles her cheek like a feather or a fine paint brush, and everything is dark, immobilised, like she's no longer in control of her own body, time to wake up, time to wake up, but it's not working and she wants to scream but all that comes out is a retch that echoes into the never ending darkness.*

***

The nest appeared on the first morning of my retreat. I didn't notice it initially, nestled in a nook in the corner as if hiding a tiny mouse hole. It was made, as nests usually are, with broken twigs, brittle and dry, woven into a labyrinthine basin. No eggs were inside, nor feathers or hint of usual habitation. Instead, there were tiny pebbles, white and smooth and shiny. I picked them up one by one and counted them. Thirty-two in total.

Odd.

I checked the window to make sure there were no gaps. Like many old buildings, the panes were at an angle, so that the wood creaked, and the hinges rattled. But the only spaces between were tiny air pockets that were just big enough to let a spider through.

The sun was still low in the sky and the clouds were painted a rusty orange. The view from the window was even more idyllic than it had been the night before—a craggy cliff overlooking an endless ocean, exactly the kind of escape I'd wanted to finish the last piece of my collection.

I looked down at the nest again. *It's an old house*, I thought. It must have been there the night before, and I hadn't noticed because it was dark when I'd arrived. I scooped it up carefully, cradled it in my hands and felt the surface of the pebbles again. A stabbing pain shot to my jaw and I clenched it. I really needed to go to the dentist about that wisdom tooth when I got home.

I took the nest outside and left it on the picnic bench, then set myself up in the living room. Placing a sheet on the floor, I angled my easel in the middle, facing the window so that I could see the trees behind the cottage move back and forth in their secret whisper outside. No one would disturb me here. I propped the blank canvas up and tried to summon a creative image in my mind. Shapes began to form, so I picked up the palette—selecting black, white, blue, and emerald-green—and started painting wherever the brush took me.

By the end of the day, I'd barely finished the background, but the outline of something was starting to take form—splashes of colours danced amidst blurry edges.

Later, as I made dinner, I glanced out to the garden and saw the nest sitting there in the soft light of the moon. Something about it was making me curious, like an itch I needed to scratch. So, I took it back inside and washed the pebbles in the sink until they were shiny and polished. Back at my easel, I stared at the dashes of colour in front of me. I knew there had been something missing—the pebbles were the perfect addition, so I stuck them on carefully with glue and paint. A beak had formed.

***

She's surrounded by bright light and she can't make a sound for it's as if her mouth has been sewn shut, and it's still and quiet here, lying on her back facing the light, then in the brightness a flash of black and white plumage breaks through and she can just make out a bird—a magpie—soaring towards her, and it lands, starts to dance on her abdomen, searching, as if trying to find a worm, though it's alone, solitary, so she tries to salute it, but her arms are stuck, the sorrow will come, and now it's jumping on her stomach, the talons digging into flesh, she screams, it hurts so much, digging and digging, and then from its beak she sees what looks like a worm, covered in red and white, and the magpie looks at her with a tilted head, a blink of its green-grey eyes, and it jumps away, flying into brightness.

***

It appeared again the next morning. This time it lay on the windowsill as I looked out into the bright breaking haar across the sea. I couldn't be sure if it was the same nest, but it was in the same intricate shape. I peered inside expecting pebbles again, but instead a piece of rope, curved and twisted, was curled up in the centre. It was covered in red dirt and stringy fibres as if it had only recently been dug up from the earth. What sort of creature collects pieces of rope? I opened the window and lifted it inside.

The rope was rough in my hands, fibres bristling against my skin. It felt oddly familiar, as if it were a missing piece to some puzzle I didn't understand. My stomach twisted like a flutter of wings and grumbled angrily at me. I took the rope with me as I went downstairs, soaking it in the sink so that the water turned red. After I'd finished my breakfast, the rope had bulged out in size, so I left it to dry on the aga while I worked.

As the day wore on, the painting wove with colour. My hand seemed to move of its own free will, colour cresting and twisting like crashing waves. Slowly a body started to appear, then a beady eye, and an ivory stomach. But I just couldn't get the feet right.

I sat back and stared at the painting until it grew dark outside. I looked at the pebbles that formed the beak and had an idea. The rope was dry, so I started to pluck at the threads, pulling bits off and positioning them beneath the stomach, until talons appeared, sharp and deadly. In the dim light of the room, they looked almost like they were moving, as if they could reach from the canvas at any moment. Satisfied, I covered the paint palette in film. I'd leave the wings for the next morning.

***

She's lying on her front while a creature pecks at her back, but she can't see what it's doing, it just pulls and digs, a euphoric pain ebbs into her body, and the skin and muscle peels away until bone is reached, and she feels the tug then, like she's being ripped apart and suddenly the pain is too much, but she can't move her arms to bat the bird away, it simply digs relentlessly until it extracts the piece it needs, and she feels a deep ache in her lungs as if the cage protecting them has been broken, and the darkness comes swift and unyielding.

***

On the third morning, I found the window open, even though I was sure I had shut it the night before. I shivered, feeling my way around the room, searching for any hint of intrusion. But there was, of course, none. Maybe the next retreat should be somewhere less remote, though I did enjoy the freedom this place gave me—it allowed me to be absorbed by my painting, to really give myself to the art. The end result was always better that way.

It was a bright day for the start of autumn, and light spilled in through the sash windows of the kitchen when I ventured downstairs. But something caught my eye as I was filling the kettle. Sitting on the armchair, resting on the soft cushion was a nest. It was a little bigger than before, to accommodate the item within. A piece of driftwood, white and hollow and curved, lay safely within its walls.

As I leant down to inspect it closer, a pain shot into my ribs and I had to steady myself on the armrest. The moment passed quickly—I blamed the mattress for being too soft. I picked up the driftwood carefully. It was light and felt smooth like porcelain. I set it down on the table and realised its shape was odd, thin at one end and thick at the bottom with little ridges jutting out—almost like a broken wing without its feathers.

My mind wandered to my incomplete painting, knowing this was the perfect part. Ignoring the now-whistling kettle, I took the driftwood and presented it to my canvas. It slotted in perfectly beneath the curved black plumage, the flash of emerald-green tail, the rope feet and the pebbled beak. After I had glued it on, I drew the final line, connecting the beak to the tail.

And I felt a deep ache in my muscles. My head spun as the room moved. I tried to steady my breathing, but it was no use—I was already falling.

***

The world is blurry again as she feels like her body is being pulled apart, piece by piece, limb by limb and reconstructed into a strange whole, and she can't breathe as the morphing continues, all she wants is for it to stop, she can't open her eyes and there's just a constant stabbing pain of stretching and pulling and compressing and she's shrinking, her body itches with strange barbs bristling out of her, until all she can do is curl into a ball and let the night take her.

***

I'm awake, though something feels off. Moonlight drifts through the panes and there's a whistle of air in the room. But the space is too big for me and everything looks out of perspective. I blink and look up at the bed. A figure is lying there, sleeping. My mind is foggy, like I'm still in a dream.

I glance at my feet and clawed talons stretch out. Underneath them is a nest that looks oddly familiar, broken twigs knotted together into a labyrinthine structure. But it's empty, and a nest shouldn't be empty.

I'm drawn towards the sleeping figure, a woman with gleaming hair. There's a paint set by her bed, clean, shiny, and untouched. A clock ticks slowly, second by second. Then it stills and all I can hear is the sound of her breathing. Her mouth is open, a gaping maw with walls of glittering moonlit silver—thirty-two pebbles in a row. Just the parts I need. I lean in and pluck the pebbles out, one by one, placing them carefully in the nest. After, I gaze upon the creation, feeling a warmth in my beak.

I push the nest into the corner by the window and hop up to the sill. A chill wind ruffles my feathers. But it will be sunrise soon. I'll come back tomorrow, and the next day, to work on my creations, nesting, until my collection is done.

Lyndsey is an Edinburgh-based writer and Scottish Book Trust New Writers Awardee. Her work has been featured in several anthologies and magazines, and in audio drama format with the Alternative Stories and Fake Realities *podcast. She's currently working on her debut novel. Find her on Twitter (@writerlynds) or via www.lyndseycroal.co.uk.*

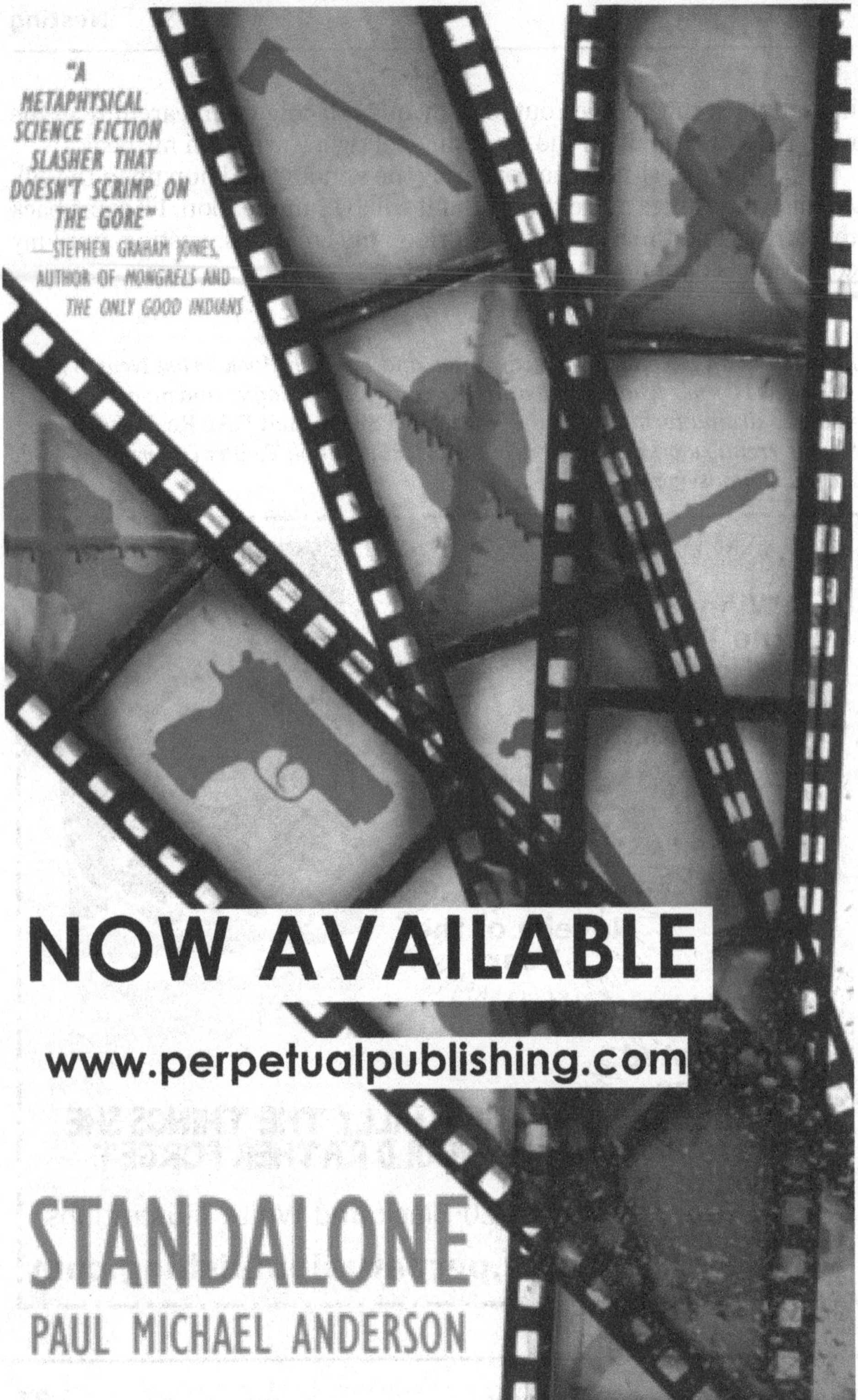
"A METAPHYSICAL SCIENCE FICTION SLASHER THAT DOESN'T SCRIMP ON THE GORE"
—STEPHEN GRAHAM JONES, AUTHOR OF MONGRELS AND THE ONLY GOOD INDIANS
NOW AVAILABLE
www.perpetualpublishing.com
STANDALONE
PAUL MICHAEL ANDERSON

COME CELEBRATE ALL THINGS SPOOKY.

Twitter @GhoulishPod
www.ghoulishpod.com

Listen on your favorite podcast app!

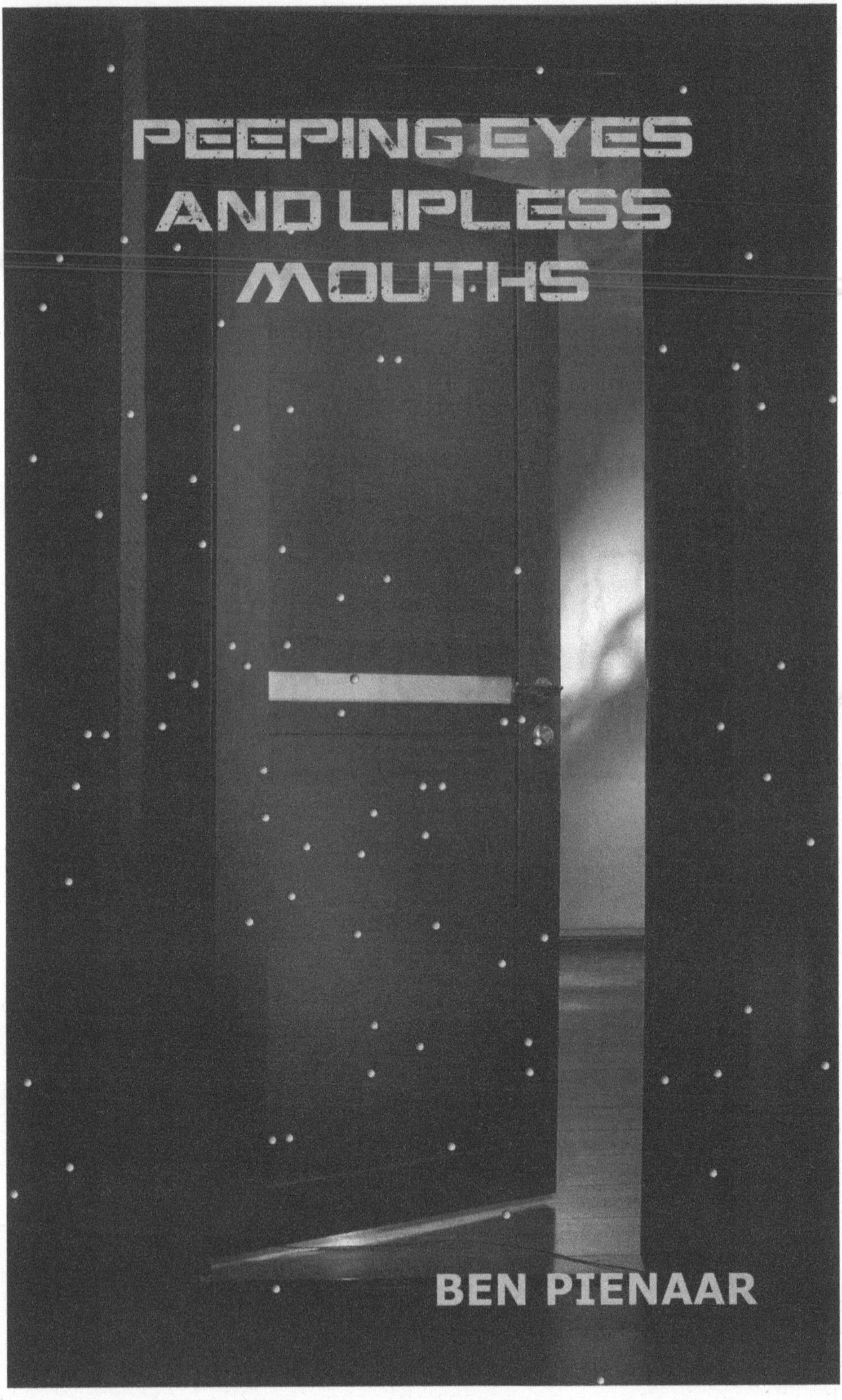
PEEPING EYES
AND LIPLESS
MOUTHS
BEN PIENAAR

THE HOUSE, he could have lived with. Even with its rats in the walls, its moss-like carpets that soaked every drop of moisture and never let go, its claustrophobic architecture and cracked ceilings. He could live with the constant thickness in the back of his throat, and the fact that even lying in bed under three blankets, he could see his breath most mornings. And he could live with his shit car and his boring job.

But what George Ambrose was finding, every day now, was that the one thing he would not be able to live with much longer was Pauly Ford.

***

George had met Pauly right here in this dog kennel of a house. George's work friends were there, plus about a half dozen hangers on including Pauly himself, and they were all sitting around the pool table that dominated the living room. Pauly had been hilarious—dancing on the table and doing a perfect handstand at one point. He'd had everyone enthralled one moment—with an intense discussion about his theories on alien life among us—and rolling on the ground with laughter the next.

When George overheard him talking about needing a place to stay, he jumped on it. At the very least there'd be no fear of romantic involvement this time. After Elyse, George was sure he never wanted to talk to a human female ever again. Pauly would shake him out of his misery and pay the other half of the rent, which was already starting to tear giant holes in George's bank account.

It was a match made in heaven.

And at first, it was. But Pauly . . . well, the problem was, the same chaotic element that made Pauly fun at parties also made living with him a nightmare.

He didn't, or couldn't, clean anything. Despite hardly owning any material goods, he left everything he had, and plenty of junk food bags and bottles besides, all over the house. Music blared from his room during the night, and during the day it was some podcast about supernatural phenomena. And of course, the rich grassy smell of weed, day and night, though at least that masked the natural stenches emanating from the carpet.

***

George dared, after six months, to enter Pauly's Den. It was the last room at the end of the hall. Should have been far enough away for George to block out the sound of punk rock bands from the eighties, but it was one in the morning and he had to be up at six and he couldn't take it anymore.

He stood in front of the crooked door for a minute, wringing his hands. George had never been good at confrontation. In fact, it gave him almost physical pain to say 'no' to someone for any reason. Then he heard Pauly let off a peal of laughter—way too loud at this time of night—and the spurt of annoyance he felt was enough to spur him to action. He banged hard on the door.

'Hol' up!' A few rattles and bangs, and then the door was yanked open, releasing a cloud of tear-inducing smoke. Pauly blinked at him, surprised to see him there as if George wasn't the only other person living there.

What the hell, I'm trying to sleep! 'Uhh, hey man. What're you doing? It's like, one am?' Pauly scratched his messy beard, then turned to look back into his room as though asking himself *hey yeah, what* was *I doing?* Then he flashed George a stupid grin. 'Dude, you wouldn't believe me if I told you.'

Clearly, he'd mistaken George's irritation for genuine curiosity.

Whatever, can you just keep it down? I gotta wake up early. 'What does *that* mean?'

George hated himself as soon as he spoke the words, but miraculously they seemed to work: Pauly stepped back into his room and turned the sound lower on his laptop. Then he waved George inside.

George stepped gingerly over a pile of university assignment papers, six used mugs, and a stack of books. The cover of the one on top was a picture of the galaxy with a title in red block letters: *The Science of the Multiverse—We Are Not Alone.*

'Dude, I found this guy totally by accident. He makes videos on the dark web, because the government's been after him for like a decade. Wait 'till you hear it. It'll blow your mind.'

While he searched his computer, George took in the rest of the den. *It's like a nest*, he thought. *The nest of the most fucked up animal in existence.* The walls were mostly invisible, the surface of every piece of furniture piled so high with junk you'd need a chairlift to reach the peaks. Half of it was wires, the other half coffee-stained textbooks, baggies of weed with papers, and too many lighters to count. But by far the most bizarre detail of this panorama was a piece of paper sticky-taped to the wall above Pauly's bed. On it was an incomprehensible mess of symbols, patterns, and numbers, dotted with red watercolour.

Pauly paused the video on his laptop and turned to see George looking. 'Oh yeah, that's part of it, too,' he said. 'Dude, no ritual is complete without a little blood, right?' he raised his left hand, which had a fresh cut along the palm, and giggled obscenely. So, not red watercolour after all.

Holy shit, you're insane. Get out of my house, you weirdo. 'Ritual? Are you serious?'

Pauly nodded, then pointed to the screen, in which a gaunt man in a suit addressed the camera. 'I know it sounds crazy, but wait 'till you hear this guy's story.'

The next ten minutes were some of the most bizarre of George's life. He listened to the man, whose deep voice he immediately recognized after hearing it for hours at a time down the hall, talk about multiple universes and ancient rituals. The man described the existence of infinite dimensions, and then told a story of how he'd found ways to open windows into some of them and learn secrets of existence. According to him, these secrets had allowed him to become rich, evade the government, and see into the future.

When it was over, Pauly turned it off, leaned back in his chair and swivelled to stare at George with bugging red eyes. 'Like, mind blown, right?'

George coughed out some more smoke and massaged his temples. *I hate you.*

'Yeah, that's how I feel, too. So I been following some of his instructional videos about how to like, open little windows into another dimension. It's really complicated, though, you have to make sure you target the right dimension because some of them are dangerous, and all those symbols and shit on that paper? It has to be like, *precise*. Like, *orderly*. Really interesting.'

'Huh. I mean, that's crazy, man. I'm gonna have to think about that. Totally changed how I looked at the world. Can . . . um. Reason I came in here, though, it's really loud and I was trying to sleep, is it okay if you keep it down?'

His heart skipped a beat as he imagined Pauly reeling off into some psychotic rant. But no, all he got was a goofy smile and a 'sure man, sleep tight.' And, for once in what seemed like weeks, the house was quiet. *Thank God.*

***

It was quiet again the next day, too—oddly quiet. George would have thought Pauly wasn't there at all if he hadn't heard him go to the toilet a couple of times. The next day was the same, and George found that the joy of silence was fading fast. What the hell was Pauly *doing* in there all day? Had he taken off work? Normally he left the house from one to nine in the evening to work at the bottle shop, but George was certain he hadn't left the house in . . . three, four days now?

He came out for meals, but only at odd hours of the night, every time leaving what he used around the kitchen sink as though to say *don't worry, I'll get around to it.* The most annoying part about that was that he wasn't lying—he *would* get around to it. But only when there were no more plates to eat off in the house, and then he would only wash the single plate and cutlery he intended to use for the next meal. So, George did it instead every morning, and by the fourth day he wasn't even feeling mad about it, just concerned for Pauly's mental health.

And then one quiet afternoon near the end of that week the music blared to life, so suddenly that George jumped and dropped the glass he was rinsing. 'Shit! What the hell?' But he could hardly hear himself—it sounded like the worlds wildest party was going on in Pauly's room. After his heart returned to its normal rate and he'd cleaned up the glass, he decided he'd waited too long. He was going to have to find out what was going on now.

The walk down the hall filled him with dread. The hall was dark down at the end, except for the sliver of light beneath Pauly's door, which was an off-red. Like a darkroom. Fuck. He's doing some kind of satanic ritual or something in there. The music didn't help, either—George vaguely recognized it as Kid Cudi's 'Day n Night'. The melancholy rhyme seemed oddly appropriate.

Standing there with his hand poised to knock, George saw the holes for the first time.

They were small—smaller than cigarette burns, which is what he mistook them for at first. Perfectly round and perfectly black. They huddled near each other, trailing out from the doorframe along the hallway wall like a tendril. As soon as he spotted the first, George saw two more, one tracking along the ceiling and another on his right just above the skirting board.

The dread that had felt so thick before vanished, replaced by an anger both sudden and intense. This was the last straw. The injustice, the stupidity! Didn't Pauly realise this was going to lose them the bond, for fuck's sake? For what? Some insane idea that he could poke a hole into another dimension?

Once again riding the comforting wave of rage, George didn't bother to knock. He gripped the door handle and pushed it open, not caring what he would find now, just knowing it was going to be bad, and knowing also that he was done with Pauly from this point forward.

Even with his nerves steeled like that, it was bad. He froze in the doorway, just as Pauly's bearded face whipped around from where he was crouching on his bed by the back wall.

The wall: covered in holes. Dozens, no—*hundreds* of them—uniform black circles that tessellated like honeycomb. And, like the honeycomb, it seemed to buzz with life. As though there were things living in the holes, sliding and twitching just out of sight in those far reaching wells. The effect was made doubly worse by the red wax candles that were dripping on every flat surface in the room, including the carpets.

Whatever there was to see, it appeared Pauly had been getting an eyeful: when he looked around George saw that he had red marks on his face like he'd been wearing goggles for a long time. Then he realised they were a result of having his face pressed to the wall. Where his face had been, there were two holes that were slightly larger than the others, giving the impression of that odd cluster of eyes usually belonging to spiders. Pauly had been peering through those holes like a pair of binoculars.

'Dude,' Pauly said, grinning. 'You gotta see this.'

The idea of pressing his face up against those holes in the wall to look through was utterly horrifying to George, although he couldn't have said why. After all, Pauly's back wall was nothing but thin plasterboard on a pinewood structure. The holes couldn't have been more than five inches deep or they would have just opened straight out into the back garden. Only, with a degree of certainty that was as much a mystery to George as the holes themselves, he knew they *were* deeper. Much, much deeper.

Thankfully, there was plenty of rage boiling inside him to dispel the fear. It was the candles: there had to be at least ten, packed into that tiny room which was filled with so much paper, scrunched up receipts and junk food bags and wooden furniture. How, *how* could someone do this?

'In the morning?' George said, keeping his voice level with some effort. 'I'm gone, okay? You can find a new roommate.'

There should have been some kind of outburst. Surely Pauly understood how impossible it would be to find someone to move in and pay rent for this junk heap? But before George had even finished the sentence, Pauly had already turned back to the wall, pressing his eyes against those binocular holes again. 'Amaaaaaazing,' he said in a whisper.

George shook his head in disgust, but he was also aware of a sudden and powerful urge to push Pauly away from the wall and look, see for himself. *It's just a prank he's playing. There are no other dimensions, just holes in a stupid wall.*

So he turned and left. The last thing he heard was another breathless sigh from Pauly: 'It's so . . . big, out there,' he said. 'So empty.'

***

George had not applied to any other junk heaps recently, but that was okay because Shirley from his work needed someone to move into her junk heap and it turned out to be even cheaper than where he was living with Pauly. Shirley was a tangled knot of insecurities, depression, and health problems, but she was funny and she said George could move in with her and her friend Allen Harper the very next day.

Standing in a driveway that was more weed than concrete, holding two fat suitcases of luggage (his furniture was all in Ikea boxes in his car, except for the old mattress that rode on the roof), George reminded himself why he was doing this. Still. It was bad.

There was barely any furniture inside. One table with a couple of chairs in the kitchen; a large screen TV sitting on the hardwood floor in what could barely be called a living room. Cushions replaced couches. Mattresses lay on the floor instead of beds. The stains, mould and rats that had plagued his previous house were also here in abundance. At least the company was good.

They were both drug addicts, he learned. Shirley seemed surprised that he didn't know, his eyes bugging out of his head when she pulled out a syringe in front of him. 'Oh, shit, you're like, clean? I thought for sure you were like . . . you know?' She giggled. Allen was already passed out with a box of cheap Moscato emptied beside him.

'No, I mean, I've never tried, you know, just weed and alcohol. I'm not judging.'

'Oh, okay. You wanna try? Don't have to shoot it, I got some pills in my drawer.'

George politely declined and then watched, masking his horror as best he could, as she injected herself and an expression of extreme bliss passed over her face. She closed his eyes and laid back against the wall. 'Yeah well lemme know ifyou chain your mine.'

The rest of the night, George sat on the edge of his mattress in his bare bones room, thinking about the choices he'd made in his life, and then thinking about Pauly, and the holes. The way they'd made him feel. The potential they'd seemed to hold . . . but for what, he couldn't say. Nothing good.

He fell asleep cold and lonely, but grateful to have left.

***

Two days later, Pauly called him. He sounded sick, or badly hungover. His words weren't quite slurred, but they sounded badly put together, as if someone had broken a few teeth or fractured his jaw. His voice came through uncomfortably loud and fake-enthusiastic over the phone.

'HEYYYYY The G Meister!'

'Pauly? Why are you calling me? I paid out everything, I left, okay? There's nothing left to sort out.'

'Uuuuuuuhhh. Yeah, so listen man. I need you to get over here, okay, cos I got a problem and I need someone to help me get out.' Through the strange quality of his voice, George detected a shaking, as if he were nervous or afraid.

'I can't give you any money, Pauly,' he said.

'NO! No I don't want money, man. I just need . . . I just need you to drive over and park your car on Diner street, right under my bedroom window. And when I jump out, you gotta just floor it, okay? Just floor that shit with me on the roof and I'll hang on, don't even worry.'

George took the phone away from his ear and stared at it for a second.

'Pauly? What kind of drugs are you on right now?'

'Come on, man, no! Just please do this one thing I'll fucking give you anything you want I swear, I'll pay your rent for the next month or whatever. I just need this one out. There was, there's *things*. In the holes. Okay? There's things in the holes, and they're gonna get me unless I can make a quick escape.'

'Why don't you just climb out the window?' George had read somewhere that when people were hallucinating you should never tell them they're crazy but pretend their hallucinations were legitimate and talk them around by asking logical questions.

'They're too fast,' Pauly said. 'They'll drag me back in. I gotta be out and driving in two seconds. Come on come on, man, don't let me down.'

George ran a hand through his hair for what felt like the hundredth time that day. 'Fuck, all right. All right, I'll come.'

'Thankyou so much please hurr—'

George hung up.

***

When he got there, idling just below Pauly's window as promised, nothing happened. He texted *I'm here* twice and got no response. His calls went unanswered. Finally, he rolled around to the front of the house and got out.

It looked about the same as when he left it, except for one detail. There was a hole, about the size of a cigarette burn, in the middle of the front door. He bent to look through, but couldn't see anything. *Much, much deeper.*

George stood on the porch for a few minutes, indecisive. He hadn't been expecting to get out of the car, and he'd left in a rush, not taking any shoes. The thought of entering that house barefoot made him wince. But, despite Pauly's weirdness, he couldn't help but feel bad for him. All alone in that house, thinking he was being chased by monsters. And he'd been a nice guy, after all. George owed it to him to at least find out what had happened. *What if he killed himself?* Pushing the thought aside, he opened the front door and stepped inside.

Every wall, every piece of furniture, was covered in holes. They crowded together like hundreds of little bugs in a nest. They'd spread to parts of the floor and ceiling, too, but not so much that George couldn't step around them on his way to Pauly's room.

He wasn't afraid—not then—because his senses told him that the house was well and truly empty. It was too quiet. Even Pauly wasn't there, though where else he could have been George wasn't sure. Instead, he felt a keen sense of morbid curiosity. Pauly had clearly lost his mind, and George wanted to find out what it looked like when someone really, truly went mad.

The bathroom was full of holes, too, and that was as impressive as it was disturbing: how had Pauly managed to make such perfect holes in tile? In porcelain?

Then he opened the door to Pauly's room. The holes were everywhere: they even pierced Pauly's beloved laptop and desk like swiss cheese. Pauly was nowhere to be seen.

Okay, house is empty, let's go. But, there was one thing. There was one thing George couldn't quite let go. The two binocular holes had merged into one larger one, about the size of a saucer in the back wall.

It's so . . . big out there. So empty.

He wanted to look. He had to look, just to see. Just to know.

The floor was full of tiny holes, so he stepped on the piles of books and papers, and then hopped onto the bed, crawling over to the spot he'd last seen Pauly. He didn't touch the wall, but levelled his face with the hole so that he could see inside properly.

Blackness. No, not quite. Out there, so far out it was impossible, miles and miles, George saw a pale figure floating. It was Pauly. His arms and legs were spread out as if he were bound spread-eagled, although no ropes were visible. He wore jeans and a shirt, but these clothes were covered in holes, as were his bare arms and legs and face. He was screaming at the top of his lungs, though George sensed that he was only hearing it a few minutes after the fact, as if it was taking the sound that long to cross the vast expanse of blackness that separated them.

George tore away, the wall peeling reluctantly from his face as if the holes were suckers on an octopus tentacle. *When did I lean into the wall?* It was only then that he realised that there was in fact, some suction there—a current passing through the wall as the holes sucked air from the room in quiet streams.

Perhaps that was why, when he finally screamed, it sounded so far away—it was being drawn out into the blackness beyond. Perhaps Pauly would hear it in a minute or two.

The air continued to pull at George as he broke out into the hallway. Behind him, the bed groaned and creaked as something heavy folded out of one of the eye holes and landed on the old springs. George did not look back. He was fighting his way down the hallway, resenting the moss-thick carpet more than ever, his gaze fixed on the front door that might as well have been a thousand miles away.

Heavy steps thudded in his wake, accompanied by a frantic wheezing. The desperate squeals of a dog as it strained on its leash to snap up a delicious piece of fresh meat.

Almost there, now, George slipped his jacket back over his shoulders as he ran, and it was whipped away by the suction. Later, he was sure that it had blinded the thing behind him, just long enough to allow him wrench open the front door and launch himself over the threshold.

Suddenly free of the terrible suction, George practically flew across the front garden to his beaten-up Ford. Only after he'd thrown himself into the driver's seat, started the engine, and shifted into drive, did he dare glance in the direction of the house.

It looked just as destitute and deserted as it had when he arrived. The only difference was that the front door was hanging slightly ajar.

George checked his rearview mirror again just a second later as he accelerated up the street, and this time he saw that it was closed.

***

Shirley was there when he got home, uncharacteristically clearheaded and enthusiastic. Or at least, as clearheaded as someone like her could ever be. She was mixing some kind of cocktail on the kitchen counter, filled with blueberries, ice and orange wedges. Beside the mixture was an orderly array of round white pills. She hummed as she poured coconut milk into a blender.

'Heyyyy Georgie how are you today?' She said, smiling warmly, oblivious to the terror that he was sure must be written all over his face.

'I got some really good H today. Cut with sugar, so you don't have to worry about 'em being strong or anything. Sure you don't wanna try?'

George opened his mouth to tell her that he was moving out, that he was probably going to move out of state, maybe even out of country, and he was sorry but he'd send her the rent for the month from wherever he was. Then her dopey eyes moved from his face down to the floor and she cocked her head to one side, brow furrowed. 'Hey, whyn't you wear shoes? You're tracking mud in here.'

'I . . .' George had forgotten that he'd driven to Pauly's house barefoot. He'd tracked muddy footprints all over the hardwood floor. But before he could make any kind of apology, something about the prints caused the words to stick in his throat.

George had flat feet, and usually when he left footprints they came in the form of big rectangular slabs on the floor, with his stubby toes dotted at the end. But these footprints weren't uniform at all. They were broken up all along the heel and up to the balls of his feet, with a hundred tiny dots, little dry circles where mud should have been.

Just seeing it was enough to make him itch, a terrible itch on the soles of his feet that made him think of dozens of spiders crawling in and out of burrows.

'I'm sorry . . .' he said faintly, feeling as though someone else was speaking with his mouth. He gave Shirley a crooked smile of his own, eyeing the pills again. 'Maybe . . . maybe just one,' he said.

***

He never checked the bottom of his feet to be sure. He didn't have to: the holes appeared shortly on his right arm, just above the elbow, and then another behind his left knee. They never appeared in ones or twos, but always in little clusters of a dozen or so, most of them too small even to fit a needle in. But they grew over time.

The justification for the drugs was right there: George told himself they would work as a kind of medicine. If he poisoned himself, surely he could poison whatever was making the holes, the same way they used radiation to treat cancer. But the truth was, of course, the drugs merely allowed him not to feel the horror that overwhelmed him in his steadily more infrequent moments of sobriety.

The holes. More clusters appeared in the walls and floor, and even on the furniture. Neither Shirley nor Allen seemed to notice them, but then there wasn't much they did notice from beneath the fog of the narcotics.

Still, there were some moments of clarity. Like when Shirley walked in on a half-gone George trying to make himself all the way gone with a syringe in his arm. He kept missing the vein he was aiming for—his vision didn't work so well these days and he didn't want to stick the needle into one of those ready-made holes.

'Oh my God.' He looked up and saw her standing with one scrawny hand over her mouth. 'Dude, you gotta get that checked out.'

'Wha—?' He looked down at his pasty body stupidly. He wasn't wearing his shirt. So many of the clusters, some of which had already joined and expanded, had become almost normal to him. Though he tried not to look unless he was well protected by a thick wall of H around his mind. 'Oh, right. Issa skin condition don't worry bout it.'

Though a little while later, when he was swimming in a warm pool and fear was only a foreign thing felt by strangers, he took another look. The holes around his belly and intestines had enlarged, by . . . rather a lot. He could have fit his fist in the largest one. By all rights, he should have been over to look right into his own stomach and identify his last meal. But of course, not with *these* holes. These holes didn't lead where you thought they did, and George didn't like to look into them at all in case he saw something move. In his late night hallucinations he thought of them as living things: a million peeping eyes and lipless mouths.

He abandoned work, moving, life, everything except the pursuit of oblivion. Now the race had become about how soon he could end himself with drugs. It was either them or . . . well, he just didn't want to end up where Pauly was, that was all. Out there.

But the drugs were not an efficient suicide method, contrary to popular belief. No, in his sober moments he knew he should hang himself or slit his wrists, except that he didn't have the energy to get up from the bed. He felt hollow inside. *No, not quite hollow.* Sometimes in the dark hours of dawn he sensed movement from within. Something with slender limbs navigating the network of tunnels, shifting through a space more vast than earth, than space itself, approaching the surface.

And then, one restless night, woken by a powerful itching, George looked down at the enormous cavity below his chest and saw an inhuman face rising from the void within.

Ben Pienaar was born in South Africa and emigrated to Melbourne, Australia in 1999. He works in a liquor store to finance his crippling caffeine addiction, and spends his free time surfing, playing chess, and training Jiu Jitsu. His first horror novel Holly and the Nobodies *is currently available from Hellbound Books via Amazon and Kindle. His unpublished work can be found on* www.freenightmares.me

Shadows

Melekwe Anthony

YES. YES, *I wanted it but not like this. The story of my life.*

How many people really know what it feels like? To have no fear, no anxiety, just need. Want maybe, for that food that lives in another. Only few people can say they know what thrill comes with night hunting. Another could happen but basically, you kill or you get killed. That last part used to be most unlikely, but since that group of knights began to tell tales of chivalry, many foolish sheep thought it wise to challenge the wolves.

You would not understand. Even now in the dark, I secretly hope this inexperienced tough man would turn on me with a stick. I love the brave ones. But sadly, he doesn't. He walks through my alley without a care. Surely he must have heard the stories, read the papers, people go missing here and I am the cause.

I move too quickly and silent for his ordinary ears. I enjoy the stealth so much I contemplate pulling his belt and circling the bastard before I clam down on him. I come from behind. All the while he ignores the world around him as he types on his phone. I stretched my arm just over his shoulder and I tell you, I was at the verge when his right ear moved slightly.

It is not common. In fact it is rare for any human to pick my approach. The others usually realize what's happening only when I am at their throat. I retreated and watched. Only trained warriors could hear that well. If such reflexes weren't learned and perfected, it must be hereditary. Even though I have to be careful, I knew I could take him. He might be twice my human age and bulky for a divorced man with three teenagers in his care, but I'm having my fun tonight.

I know him well. It is nights like this that I justify my needs, telling myself I really do God's work, scorching the earth of these evil criminals, wife-beaters, rapists and harlots. But Mr. Johnson is even worse. He plans to sell his own daughters.

I move again behind him and whisper in one long sigh, 'Thy night has come'. On instinct, he turns back and I can see from my hidden place that his eyes are round in fear.

'Who is there?' he calls out foolishly.

Why do they ask when they don't really want to know? Is it to confirm their fears or douse them? I have never known fear but if I did, I would run now and ask later.

"It is I" I fake an accent. The words were barely out of my mouth when I realized it. *Really? It is I? You couldn't think of something else? Why not just say 'Ho! Ho! Ho!!! I bear presents?* I scold myself, yet this doesn't put him at ease. I can't imagine why.

"Show yourself. Whoever you are," he holds his arms ready for battle toward the direction of my voice.

"Okay. Let's be civil," I call from behind him. He turns too fast and almost trips on his fat legs.

"What do you want?" I can hear the fear now. Sweet prickly fear. "I haven't done shit."

"Well, you're about to and I can't let that happen." I step into the light and I can see him recover. He is probably calculating my age and he is beaming with his advantage.

"What's that supposed to mean!" His voice rises. "Who sent you? Who do you think you are following me? You've got one chance. Spill!"

He gets closer like he's going to hit me. I don't move. I don't flinch from his voice or the ugliness of his pizza-sized face. I like them brave. I allowed him a smile and I enjoyed that quick second as his bravery falters. He recovers and continues his pace. All the while I am thinking how difficult it will be to locate his pulse.

I don't always go for the jugular. Maybe the back, the arm or something of virgin flesh, but somehow, as I watch in slow motion while all parts of him shake while he comes this way, I knew I wouldn't find a pulse in any of these places.

To humans my age and my experience, they would probably describe it as 'He thundered towards me. Ground shaking and wind ceasing. All standing still to watch Goliath puddle this fly. And just like that it happened'

Mr. Johnson struck me and my face followed the trajectory. A powerful blow that could have broken a bone, if I had been human. Not what I expected from so thick a man, but I'll take it. Better than the look of fear moments ago. I love how his eyes peel back and his mouth hangs open when I turn my face back to him. Blood is not gushing down my nose and I haven't staggered from my spot. I return his gaze with a smile. He has just witnessed what I am. Strong, invincible, fast and most of all—dramatic.

That's me, Thomas Andrew Baker, Tab for short. Let's forget what happened to the traffic merchant and the gory details of how the police found him in my alley, their sixth incident this month. The girls will survive. In fact, they will do way better. All three of them used to be my neighbors and everyday I wished I could do what I did last night. After all, have you not heard that a man's life is not equal to many?

I have to leave the neighborhood. The police will begin to suspect the nature of the killings, if they haven't already. How all six victims were into shady business. How they have different quantities of blood in them—some two liters, some half, some none. How all victims were found in my alley and their time of death say past sunset. Yeah, they already suspect, but can't admit it. Humans are like that. They believe thinking or talking about my kind would simply draw me from whatever I am doing to their homes. Over-exaggerated superstitions right? But you never know, I might be close by.

Well sorry for you if you think I am being vague. If you haven't read the signs or seen the movies, let me describe myself. I am that Shadow of Shadows who Shadows fear. I am the omen by twilight and the diner in the darkness. I have had many names before—Lamia, Blood-sucker, Witch, Evil, but the most obvious you have heard, Vampire.

Once I preferred being called the un-dead, but these days that seems to quantify Zombies and Mummies, which I tell you are all works of fiction, stories told by singers and poets to become famous. I should know—I was there.

Yes, I stood there when you burned your dead fathers and sisters so they wouldn't become me, when you placed crosses at your mother's grave so she would not return. Foolish humans. Every time I dug them out to scare you, tormenting you until you went back to those graves and found blood in the mouths of their un-decaying corpses. Yes, this was me. But don't be scared, you are only human.

You claimed I died a witch and crawled out a blood sucker. You said your brothers didn't decompose, so they were part of me. Humans, if only you knew. If you knew those priests and exorcists who prayed for you weren't really normal and those who you feared were too close for your whisperings, you would never have forgotten the stories. We are many.

Melekwe Anthony is a fierce writer. His works have been published in Adelaide Literary Magazine, Pride Magazine, The Yard, Multiplicity Magazine, Salmon Creek Journal, Rigorous Magazine, the Inlandia Journal *and* Fleas On The Dog *among others. He currently writes for* Dead Talk Live, USA *and the* Hindu College Gazette.

JAY WILBURN

Is Reading Really a Pleasure?

I'M GOING TO try to talk you out of reading. It's got to be easier than talking people into reading. I mean, reading must be a chore, or it wouldn't be this much work. No one teaches people how to watch TV in school. We learn that the old-fashioned way through individual practice and parental neglect at an early age. No one has to advertise heroin. The stuff sells itself. We spend millions of dollars trying to convince people not to do stuff like that. If you want to know what is really a pleasure in life, look at the stuff people spend all their time and money trying to get people to stop doing. That's where the real joy is. So, if reading is really a pleasure, then I should be a responsible adult and try to talk you out of it.

Video is More Fun.

Of course, it is. Goes without saying. You know how to make video less fun? Make a video of an author reading to you. That will kill the buzz real fast.

When you are tired to the point that your eyes hurt after a day of work or a day of staring at a computer screen or phone, it's best to rest your eyes. Still, if your head hurts and you're exhausted, you'll sit in front of the TV and let it play. If you read, you're more likely to fall asleep sooner.

Maybe that is better for you, but arguably the thing that keeps you up into the dark hours of the morning is more fun than the thing that puts you asleep.

Some of you stay up late reading chapter after chapter, I suppose, so maybe there is some pleasure in it. Streaming is more addictive to more people, though. It is passive, less work, and can be sustained for longer. That's a good sign of what is objectively more fun.

Something pleasurable might take some work and take some practice. Sex is fun. It gets better with practice and if the partner or partners are putting in effort. It's better if you are in shape. It's better if you are healthy. It passes the test that people spend a lot of time trying to keep young people from doing it. Sex is more work than reading, but is more fun if you're doing it right. Sex and running up a flight of stairs burns the same calories. If you did both at the same time, you would more than double the calorie burn. Arguably running up a flight of stairs is more effort and less fun no matter how good you are at it.

Learning to sail a boat is fun. It requires a lot of work and effort. People are willing to spend large amounts of money on the equipment and the training. Like heroin, it is expensive, dangerous, and you have to go through dealers.

Reading requires years of schooling for many kids. Sure, some learn to read at home, but if that was working for everyone, we wouldn't bother with it in school. We have to make the reading, writing, and math school free and require it by law in order to get kids in the building. Young adults will pay for college, but the beer and sex are big incentives, and the crippling debt is in exchange for a piece of paper required for some careers.

My point is that TV is less work and more fun. People are willing to pay for books, streaming, sex, and sailing. Books are the only thing in that list that does not neatly fit the alliteration, and that bothers me. Some people would take these things for free or steal them if they could get away with it. So, this section is not conclusive on whether reading is really a pleasure.

THERE ARE TOO MANY BOOKS

There are more TV shows than you could ever watch, but you just sort of drift from one to the next. You don't really worry whether you will live long enough to watch all the shows. If anything, you hunt around looking for anything good to watch.

Books? There are too many. You won't live long enough to read all the ones you're supposed to in order to be a good person much less all the ones that might be fun to read. You get your hands on a book that's bad and you've wasted that much more of your life. Some people will read books more than once. That's a good sign that they might be fun after all, but think of all the books you won't read before you die! That's a lot of pressure.

Not Reading Makes You Feel Guilty

If you feel guilty about not getting in your reading time, can that really be a pleasure? That puts reading in the category of obligations. Reading is more like exercise, finishing your work on time, or going to church. And not like the sex kind of exercise. More like running up the stairs without having sex. That means reading is less like streaming your favorite show, playing video games, or Internet porn. Under this paradigm, reading is a chore.

Lots of people are unhappy if they haven't had sex in a while, but not because it is an obligation. It's not like they wish they had more time for sex because their parents would be disappointed in them. I suppose sex is looked at as a chore by some people too. If you're married and your partner is bad at it, but they get grumpy if you withhold it too long, so you figure you better schedule it in to keep the peace. But again, that probably means you're doing it wrong. I should really talk to my wife. See if she has a performance review for me. Things I can improve upon.

Maybe I'm doing it wrong. Reading, I mean, not the sex. I'm great at the sex. Just ask . . . okay, I don't have a lot of references, but I'm putting in the work.

Anyway, stop picturing me having mediocre sex; this is about reading.

Guilt has a weird relationship with pleasure. We feel guilty for doing some things we enjoy for a variety of reasons. We feel guilty for not doing things for a variety of reasons.

You feel guilty for not finishing a book, you feel guilty for not getting to the books you want to read, you feel guilty for buying more books when your "to be read" pile is already years-worth-of-reading high, you feel guilty for not reading books everyone thinks you should have read, and you may feel guilty about some of the books you do enjoy that the cool literary kids wouldn't approve of.

Guilt may not be a good indicator of anything.

And I sex just fine, so let it go! Okay?! Damn.

READING JUST WON'T DIE

We try to mark the decline of humanity with the decline in reading, but it keeps hanging in there. If anything, reading is expanding to more platforms. We predict that ebooks are killing print books, but print book sales keep resurging and ebooks are still reading. Authors are sneaking books and stories onto other platforms and formats, even ones not designed for reading, and there is some audience in all those places. Maybe not as much as authors would like, but enough to keep them writing. Amazon is starting Kindle-vella to get episodic serial stories in front of readers. They are doing it because Wattpad has made money with that model for years and years now. There is enough audience there that Amazon wants to gobble them up.

Then, there is you. You, the individual who is reading this article as I try to talk you out of reading. Every word you read is another failure on my part to stop you. You read even when there are more shows to stream. You read even though the world is full of porn and heroin just waiting for anyone who wants it. You read for all your own reasons. You want to learn something, what you are reading makes you laugh, you go on emotional journeys from page to page, you are transported to other worlds in your mind, and nothing has succeeded in stopping you.

You really may have a problem. I suppose that meets all the criteria for pleasure I've laid out in the article. I'll concede the point even though reading is still a weird thing to do with your time.

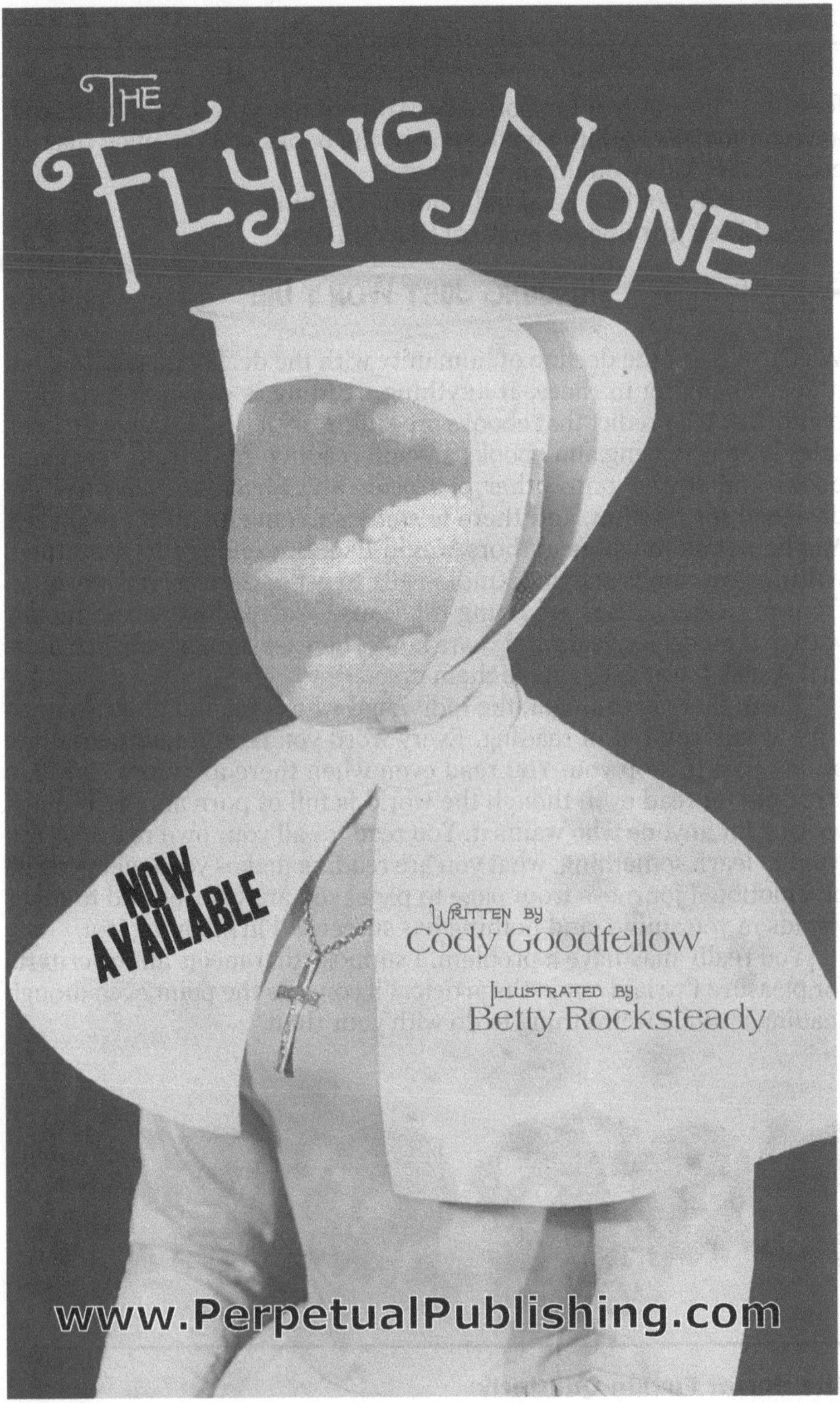
THE FLYING NONE
NOW AVAILABLE
Written by
Cody Goodfellow
Illustrated by
Betty Rocksteady
www.PerpetualPublishing.com

The Matters of Faith Podcast

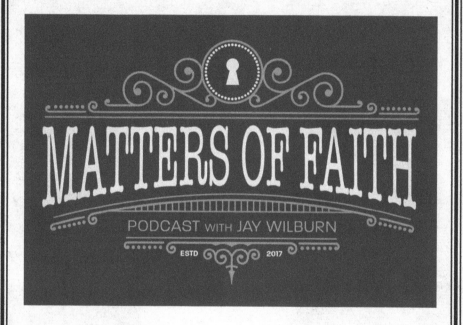

WITH YOUR HOST
Jay Wilburn

ON THE
Project Entertainment Network.

K.Y. CARTER

My Sweet Summer Child

THE SKY SMELLED dangerous; the acrid sting of trees burning, and salt. Lightning shredded the sky and clouds choked out the last drop of sunlight—Eloise knew it was time to return home. She looked down at her woven basket, picking through blue-green blooms and red-thorn stems with tiny hands. She hoped she had enough. The first growl of thunder shook the air as she closed the latch to the garden. Last time she forgot to close it she got twenty lashes, one for every radish the rabbits ate. Eloise would take her lashings quietly, watching the flames crackle in the hearth. She was a distracted child. Those who saw her said she was marked. They kept their distance, but Eloise didn't mind. She would count the clouds in the sky as her mother, Serine, would pick out meat and spices for supper. Until the other women in town began to whisper. Until they watched Eloise with those looks. Looks that reminded Eloise of the first time she squeezed a toad between her stubby fingers. The skin-crawling squish. Soon the shops began to close their doors to the two, then the town closed their boarders. Serine would miss the buzz of society, but Eloise liked the solitude of their cottage, it was quiet. There were no whispers. There she was a seven-year-old girl, not a monster— not a squished toad.

Eloise tucked her basked under her arm and began sucking on the knuckle of her index finger—a nervous habit she was never able to break. It tasted of copper and soil, and meant danger was near. Serine always watched for when the crooked bone met Eloise's lips. She would watch the tall grass for a mad fox, the stone walls for cracks, the moors for wandering travelers—whatever taboo it could be. Serine would watch with motherly eyes, with fearful eyes, with hateful eyes, for Eloise was never wrong. Out by the gardens with her basket of herbs, Eloise was alone. The only sign of her mother was a plume of smoke waving from behind the hill. So Eloise sucked her knuckle unaware, dreaming of what was to be for supper.

Climbing over the hill, bare feet holding tight to the grass, Eloise counted the seconds between rumbles. The storm was close. The wind ruffled her powder blue dress, exposing her dirty knees. Eloise knew not to kneel on her dress in the garden, it was supposed to stay blue because blue cost money. At least that was what Serine said. Serine did not know

Eloise wore the blue dress to the garden. Eloise was excited to show her she was responsible—that she did not dirty her blue dress. Eloise knew she had to be home before the rain started, or her caution was all for not.

In her own world, sniffing the water in the air, Eloise did not see the man in the barn. Serine's makeshift hut of scrapped plywood and used nails. Eloise did not see him see her. How he mirrored her sniffs, how he floated with the waves of her blue dress. Serine would have called him the spotty owl—Eloise would have called him the corn snake. Both would have been wrong. As Eloise reached the top of the hill, looking down at the rough pile of stone she called home, the man crept from his hiding place. The soft grass muffled his careful footsteps. He moved slowly, whispering to himself *please don't run.*

Eloise did not scream when she was lifted off the ground by two thick arms. The arms did not hold her tight—if it was Serine, she might have thought it was a hug, but Serine never hugged Eloise. Her legs dangled as she tried to wiggle from his grip, and Eloise was pulled back to the barn. Still, she did not scream. The man was happy about that. Eloise watched her basket on the grass, how it toddled in the wind. She willed it to stay put, to wait for her to come back. *Please don't fall over.* The man sat her down next to a sack of flour, and peeked between the splintering wood. She popped back up like a Spring daisy, eager to get back to her basket, sucking her knuckle trying to reach the sweet center. The man pushed her back down. He told her she needed to sit and listen. So she sat, but she didn't know how to listen. Her mind was clouded with thoughts of her basket, the flowers floating away on the breeze.

She didn't listen as he told her his tale—who he was, where he came from, who she was, what Serine had done. Eloise was too busy counting the petals in her mind as they danced back to the garden where she would have to pick more. When the man asked if she understood why he was there, she nodded still sucking her knuckle. The last time she got caught not listening, she got lashings. She did not listen often and was very tired of lashings. She was glad he did not ask her to repeat what he had said. The man smiled down at her on the barn floor. His eyes were soft and kind, so Eloise smiled back. The kind eyes felt warm—she couldn't place why they were familiar. Like from a dream far, far away. Eloise studied them closely, and this time she heard him. *How I have missed you my sweet daughter.* She shook her head, frizzy curls floating in a halo around her. Eloise did not like his words. Eloise did not have a father, she had a mother. Eloise did not like liars, so she felt it was time for her to leave.

She stood and dusted her bottom, hoping the blue dress was not dirty. When she stood he opened his arms for an embrace, but Eloise was walking to the door, not into his arms. The man closed his fist, slamming his arms to his sides. The man's eyes were no longer kind. He barked words Serine pretended not to use, words Eloise was told were not ladylike. *Did you hear nothing I have said? I thought you understood, that woman is evil.* Eloise turned slowly, cocking her head to one side as though she was listening for something far away. The word evil bounced in her mind. She wondered who was evil. *She stole you from me. My sweet girl. You are mine.* Eloise belonged to Serine, Serine was her mother. Eloise decided the man who claimed to be her father was mad, completely bonkers like the hatter in her favorite book. She continued to the door as he shouted behind her *You are mine, you are my child and she stole you from me. Has she already corrupted your mind with her lies? That woman is cursed.*

Curses aren't real, Eloise knew that. Serine had told her this when bad things would follow them. At home it was safe, there were no bad things. At home. *My dear girl. I shall save you, please let me. It is the least I can do. I shall save you. That witch won't hurt you anymore.* Eloise smiled to herself as she pictured Serine with magic. The cottage cleaning itself, the fire never going out, the garden safe from rabbits and voles. It would have been nice perhaps, but witches only lived in bedtime stories and dreams. That was what Eloise was thinking before the air went cold, before her chest burned with pain. Eloise thought she might have been angry. Serine had told her anger feels like a fire, and that is what Eloise felt as she shuffled through the barn door. Her legs were slow and heavy, she had only moved like this in her dreams.

Before her eyes the sky broke open and the world was blurred. Eloise thought about her blue dress. It was going to get wet and she would get lashings, but she had to get home. She picked up the fabric in her small fingers as she walked into the rain. The chill seeped into her bones, but her chest was still on fire. She looked down to see if she was burning, only to find her dress was no longer blue, it was red. Bright scarlet. Starting from her chest, the color spread across the cotton fibers. Eloise did not understand how the man had changed the color of her dress. She couldn't think, her mind was fuzzy. *Am I drowning?* She looked up to the sky as her breathing became struggled gargles. *What is going on? I need to get home; mother will know how to fix it.* In the distance she saw her basket, now toppled over, flower petals floating down the hill. Eloise tried to run to them, to catch them before they floated away. Her legs did not want to listen, she already had no breath, and soon she was on the ground. Blood and rain turned the earth below her into mud, and her powered blue dress now dirty. *Mother will be angry with me.*

K.Y. Carter holds a BA in creative writing from Columbia College Chicago. She discovered her love of writing when she decided that the heroes always winning was boring and predictable. She enjoys writing contemporary, thrillers, and speculative fiction. Her favorite part of story writing is deciding who dies.

NOW AVAILABLE!

THE GIRL IN THE VIDEO

MICHAEL DAVID WILSON

www.perpetualpublishing.com

THE MERCY SEAT: STORIES FROM DEATH ROW

We are seeking empathetic short stories that fall into the crime fiction genre told from the perspective of people on death row. The anthology will be published sometime in early 2022, and 50% of the net proceeds will be donated to an anti-death penalty charity to be determined later (We have several potential organizations in mind, but we can't advertise their involvement until first getting permission, which we are trying to do!).

To make the theme even more annoyingly specific: we want every story to be told in first-person POV, from the person currently on death row, as they tell us how they landed there. It's up to each writer whether or not their narrator is innocent of their convicted crimes. I am looking for a healthy mix of both. Stories also do not have to necessarily be set in the present. The death penalty has been around for . . . a while. Feel free to get creative with your time settings.

BIPOC and LGBT+ writers are especially encouraged to submit.

Deadline: September 1, 2021
Word count: 1,000 - 7,000
Payment: $0.05 per word
Simultaneous submissions: No
Multiple submissions: No
Reprints: No

Writers should submit their stories to storiesfromdeathrow@gmail.com with TITLE_LAST NAME_WORD COUNT in the subject line. Doc and docx files are preferred. Any questions about the project can be directed to the same address with QUERY in the subject line.

You can read the full guidelines over on LitReactor at https://litreactor.com/news/now-accepting-submissions-the-mercy-seat-stories-from-death-row

GoodNeighbor.com

JEFF WOOD

GoodNeighbor.com™
Welcome to the neighborhood!

James D: Remember, the HOA has a meeting on Thursday for everyone in the Blue Oak subdivision. We'll discuss dues, neighborhood watch, and drop-off times and locations for our dumpsters for Spring cleaning.

>Jerry C: Thanks, **James D**, for arranging for the dumpsters. I'll be there! I want to bring up planning for the community garden too.

>James D: Happy to help, Jerry. See you there! Great game last night!

>*3 other comments*

Sondra E: Has anyone seen my little Inky? He's a five-month-old cute little black cat and he hasn't been home for two nights! I miss my little furbaby! Let me know if you see him.

>Jim K: So sorry **Sondra E**. We will keep an eye out.

>Alyx C: Poor little furbaby! We'll be on the lookout for him!

>Lynn D: **Sondra E** don't you know better than to let your cats go outside? It's so cruel. All my furbabies are indoor kitties. There's coyotes and bears out there! Perverts! Satanists!

>Denise P: And they kill poor birds! Shame on you!

>*15 more comments*

Chrissy T: Hi neighbors! I'm new to the Blue Oak subdivision. Does anyone know anything about the house at the corner of Hawk Marsh Dr and Carrol Ave? I never see anyone enter or leave, but it's not for sale or anything. I live a few doors away, and I'm worried about vandals and drug users.

>Jennie C: I'm down the street, I'll keep an eye out, we have kids and don't want those kind around.

>John M: I live next door and I haven't seen anyone either.

>Lynn D: **Chrissy T** Why don't you keep your blinds shut and quit spying on your neighbors?

>Chrissy T: **Lynn D** I'm not spying, I'm looking out for the neighborhood.

>Lynn D: **Chrissy T** I for one do not want to have anyone looking out for me.

>James D: **Chrissy T** Me neither.

>*5 other comments*

Jim S: Anyone notice more missing pets on this app lately? Seems like every day someone posts that they're missing a pet. Lots of signs on telephone poles too.

>James D: Please do not clutter up telephone polls with missing pet posters, people. That's what the bulletin board is for.

>Jim S: The bulletin board is behind glass and locked.

>James D: Mail it to me or leave it at my house and I will put it up.

>Jim S: Oh great, so you get to decide what is allowed to go on the bulletin board and what doesn't?

>*17 more comments*

Sara S: Thanks **James D** for hosting the HOA meeting last night. I just wanted to say that our next door neighbor has lost two cats in the last year. She'll come to the next meeting.

>Doug R: I didn't post it here, but we lost a dog last year.

>Sue T: Us too, we lost two cats in our three years in this neighborhood.

>Lynn D: **Sue T** you are so cruel to let your cats outside. My babies never leave the house!

>Sondra E: **Lynn D** don't you have anything better to do than preach to your neighbors?

>*23 more comments*

Jeanie C: **Crissy T,** remember that house you were asking about? Where no one enters or leaves? I don't think the electricity is on. I take a nightly walk with my husband, and the lights are never on there. There's a sprinkler system, but the lawn's all dead. My husband wanted to go up and look through the window, but I wouldn't let him.

>Crissy T: **Jeanie C**, thanks for checking!

>Doug R: **Jeanie C** you might want to check with the city, they'll tell you if anyone owns the house. It's public record. Tax assessor's office, I think.

>*2 more comments*

Susan P: Our poor little Toby ran away last night! Our little boy is missing. White chihuahua/poodle mix. If anyone has seen him please contact me.

>Lynn D: Don't leave you animals outside! It's so cruel!

>Susan P: We didn't! He's an indoor dog. But he was scratching at the kitchen door all night. He heard something in the empty house next door. I went out and checked and didn't see anyone. But little Toby got so agitated he broke through the screen door and ran off!

>Alyx C: Poor little Toby! We'll keep an eye out!

>*1 more comment*

Annie P: Did anyone else see all the crows yesterday? There was a bunch of crows all over the corner of Hawk Marsh and Carrol. Settled on all the trees and roofs and electric lines. It was creepy. I'm scared they might hurt our kids or our garden.

>David G: Murder.

>Annie P: What! Murder!?

>David G: Murder of crows. That's what they're called. Not a bunch of crows. A murder of crows.

>Annie P: **David G** quit scaring people like that! :)

>*8 more comments*

Crissy T: I called the city and after about an hour they gave me the name of the person who pays taxes on that house at Hawk Marsh and Carrol. I won't put it here, but PM me and I can give it to you.

>Allan F: Why would any of us need to know the name of the people who live there? People have a right to not leave their home. Maybe they're sick. Maybe they have a mental disorder. Leave them alone.

>Sara C: **Crissy T** After we chatted I looked at their mailbox and it matches up with the name you gave me. It looked like they had mail, but I wasn't going to check – that's against the law! But I looked in their window and I didn't see anyone. Looked like there was furniture and stuff, but it's hard to tell because the curtains are shut tight.

>Allan F: **Sara C** And you didn't think the curtains being shut tight was a sign they didn't want their privacy invaded? You didn't want to check the mail but you were fine with looking in their windows? Get a clue Sara. You are invading their privacy.

>Crissy T: And drug dealers and homeless people aren't invading my

privacy? A thief breaking into my home isn't invading my privacy? Get real Allan. I'm just trying to protect my home and my neighborhood.

>Allan F: And who will protect us from you? I'm more scared of busybodies like you than I am from the homeless.

>*19 more comments*

Sondra E: We were looking for our missing black cat, poor little Inky, and we found a dead cat just past Hawk Harsh. It was concealed in the bushes, like it was hidden on purpose. It's just disgusting that someone could be so cruel. I called animal control and they came and got it. And after I told them about all the missing animals lately, the guy said they are going to increase the police presence in the neighborhood for awhile. So if you are the one who has been killing these poor animals, WE ARE WATCHING YOU!

>Doug R: So sorry for your loss of your cat, Sondra.

>Sondra E: We're not calling him a loss yet, **Doug R**! Fingers crossed!

>Sue T: I'm sad you had to find that horrible sight Sondra! Good luck with Inky!

>*5 more comments*

Crissy T: That house on Carroll and Hawk Marsh chills me to the bone! Hiding in their house like vampires.

>Sara C: We ought to be able to know who lives there. It's our right as neighbors.

>Charles R: I've been inside there. I helped the guy with his garage door once, the door had gone off the rails. He was nice enough. Invited me in for a beer. Had a little boy, didn't see a wife or anyone else. Just him and the kid. He was nice. They were nice.

>Jim J: I've been in there too. He's not too scary. He's kind of cool. He and his boy drew this HUGE design on their driveway with chalk. It looks like, I don't know, a maze, maybe? A maze inside a circle. All these weird made up letters inside it. It looked almost occult.

>Sally F: You have some messed up priorities, **Crissy T**? He out making art with his son on the driveway and you are bitching about how their house "chills you to the bone." What, a functional family dynamic chills you?

>Diana C: **Sally F** Language!!! Kids are reading this!

>*23 more comments*

Annie P: Is anyone else seeing the crows besides me? I reported it on here a couple weeks ago but the only person who said anything was some guy trying to correct my grammar.

>Sara C: I've seen a bunch around my house too. More and more with each week. At first I thought they were migrating for the winter, but my husband says crows don't migrate. And it's not winter yet.

>David G: Murder. Of crows. That's what they're called.

>Annie P: **David G** Just stop it.

>Sara C: And I've started seeing a few dead crows on the lawns too.

>1 *more comments*

Jeff W: Hi everyone. New to the neighborhood. We had sweet little cat named Bella not come home last night. An orange and grey tabby mix. She was always such a great outdoor cat, but we think maybe she got lost because she was in a new neighborhood. Please keep your eyes out.

>Sondra E: We'll keep an eye out. We found our little stinker, Inky after two weeks! Don't give up hope!

>1 *more comment*

Jim J: I saw him! The guy who lives at Hawk Marsh and Carrol. He was out in the driveway, late at, night, in a chair, just sitting there. He was friendly. Everything seemed normal. Yeah, the lawn was a mess, all dead, a lot of weeds. Some kind of drawings all over the cement, and he had chalk dust all over him. The kid watched from the screen door. The guy kept looking back at him, like checking up on him.

>Diana C: Did the kid seem okay?

>Jim J: **Diana C** I don't know. He was really quiet. He didn't really even move. Just stood at the door and watched.

>Diana C: **Jim J** Did he seem happy?

>Jim J: I don't know. Not happy, not sad. Just kind of . . . blank. Just watching.

>3 *more comments*

James D: The dumpsters are going out early Saturday morning, Sept. 5th. Remember only people in the Blue Oak subdivision can use them. We are using the honor system, please be honorable. Please don't put trash above the level of the top of the dumpster. We'll replace the dumpsters every weekend as we fill them. No tires, no paint, no electronics, no chemicals.

>Jerry C: Thanks again! Looking forward to it.

>John W: No chemicals? What does that even mean? Water is made of chemicals. Everything is made of chemicals.

>James D: **John W** You know what I mean. No pesticides or weed killer or motor oil. Use common sense.

>*2 more comments*

Jerry V: That house on the corner? Hawk Marsh and Carroll? I live across the street. That guy comes out nearly every night. About two a.m. Every night without fail. That kid is always at the screen door. I see him because my shift ends around then. He seems pretty frail. He puts a lawn chair out in the middle of the driveway. Just looks up at the sky. Sometimes he has binoculars, but not always. At first I thought he was star-gazing. But he does it on cloudy nights too. He even does it in the rain. I've never seen him out in a storm or snow.

>Sally F: He sits out there all night? Thar sounds creepy.

>Jerry V: No, only about an hour. He's pretty harmless. He's weird, but I don't think he's dangerous.

>Sally F: What about the kid? He's there at the door the whole time? That can't be healthy.

>Dottie P: Someone should call DHS!

>Lynn D: **Dottie P** Yes they should. Sounds like a crazy meth head. I bet that kid is abused.

>Jerry V: He's not a meth head. He sits quietly in the driveway. Sometimes he draws things with chalk.

>Sally F: Sits in the driveway late at night? That's not normal.

>*15 more comments*

James D: The dumpsters are in place! Also, if you leave toys and canned goods they will be taken to a non-profit to help the needy in our community. Please donate today, even if you aren't using the dumpsters.

>Jerry C: Thanks James D!

>*3 more comments*

Sara C: I called animal control because of all the dead crows. They came by today and took 2 of the dead crows to be tested for disease. She said they'd check for poison too.

>Cloe S: Thanks for calling them, **Sara C**. Let us know what they find.

>Sara C: She also said it was probably the weather. Some freak storm in the upper atmosphere. She said she saw that happen once.

>David G: A storm killed them? I don't think so. It's poison. Someone is murdering crows.

>Sara C: Quit stirring up trouble. You don't know that. There were burns on several of the birds. Animal control said they might have flown through a thunderstorm and got hit by lightning.

>David G: Um, I'm not sure that's scientifically possible.

>12 *more comments*

Jim J: I saw him too! The guy on Hawk Marsh and Carroll. After I read **Jerry V's** post about him going outside every night at 2 a.m. to sit in the driveway, I decided to look for myself. It sounded so freaky! I had a smoke out on the porch, and watched him from around the corner. He was out there, just like you said. Middle of the driveway, in the dark, looking up at the sky. He was in the center of a giant circular drawing, like a mandala, but all cut up like a jigsaw puzzle. His boy at the screen door, watching him. Didn't look very meth-head to me. He looked pretty chill. He actually looked kind of high, but maybe that was just me. :) He had a notebook, he was reading it, writing stuff down in.

>Jerry V: Cool **Jim J**! Yeah, he seems like a harmless enough guy.

>Lynn D: He looked high?

>Todd G: All sorts of druggies moving into this neighborhood. Buying houses and growing their weed and getting high.

>Jim J: It's legal here! That's why I moved here! Nothing wrong with sitting out all high in the privacy of your own driveway.

>Lynn D: It's not legal to get high in your driveway. Kids can see you!

>Jerry V: He wasn't getting high in the driveway. He was just sitting out there.

>Lynn D: And Satanic drawings in the driveway. It was a pentagram, I know.

>Jerry V: You don't know that because it's not true.

>5 *more comments*

Susan P: They found our poor little Toby in the dumpster last night! My neighbor saw him down there and recognized him right away. He got my poor little guy out and cleaned him off and brought him to me so I could identify the body. It was Toby. His neck was broken. What kind of monster does that? Not only kills a dog, but then throws it in a dumpster. It's horrid.

>Alyx C: I'm so sorry to hear about your loss, Susan.

>Sondra E: So sad. Someday you will meet him on the rainbow bridge.

>*35 more comments*

Ernest P: I read about the guy who sits out in his driveway late at night and stares at the sky. I saw a movie once about this dragon monster who would swoop down and eat people in New York City. He lived in the Chrysler Building. The premise was, no one ever looks up, they just look straight ahead. So, no one noticed the monster.

>Jim J: Hey, I've seen that movie!

>Ernest P: All I'm saying is maybe he knows something we don't know. :)

>Jim J: Remember, the moral of the story is, always look up!

>*2 more comments*

James D: Sadly, we've had to discontinue our free dumpster program. Three dead animals were found at the bottom of the dumpster we put out on Leeland and Marsh Hawk. Two cats and a raccoon were found. Anyone with any information about these horrible acts is urged to call the police immediately. You may contact me as well, at 201-555-2515.

>Jerry C: That's awful! No one has any respect anymore. I'm sorry you had to cancel the program. It was so useful, and so generous of the HOA to provide them for free. This is why we can't have nice things!

>Lynn D: It's the drugs. I bet I know who is responsible for all this. I bet most of you do too. We've talked about him here before. Getting high out where everyone can see him. A shame. I mourn for our country.

>James D: **Lynn D** You can't go around accusing people on GoodNeighbor.com™. Call the police if you have concerns or evidence. Or call me, I'd be happy to help. But you can't just accuse people because you suspect they might be the culprit.

>Jerry V: Yes, **Lynn D**, I agree with James. I understand your worries.

I have kids too. I know it's scary out there. But you can't accuse people without any evidence. If you have some, go to the police. This is not the place.

>Lynn D: **Jerry V** You and your little club here on GoodNeighbor.com™ just go on right ahead and bury your heads in the sand. You're so sure the police will protect you. I don't have time to wait for trouble.

>James D: Please don't go out looking for trouble **Lynn D**.

>*14 more comments*

Chrissy T: Did anyone else see the police on the block last night? It was really late, like 3 a.m. There was a fight out in the middle of Carroll St. I didn't see who was involved, just three cop cars and a fire truck. The police broke if off and drove away with some people in the back of their car, but I couldn't see who it was.

>Jerry V: I saw some of it. It was across the street. I came home from work just as the second cop car was pulling up. There were two men and a woman. One of the men might have been the driveway guy we were all talking about a few days ago. I couldn't tell.

>Lynn D: Serves him right.

>James D: Serves who right, **Lynn D**?

>Lynn D: I'm just sayin, **James D**.

>Sondra E: Does anyone know what happened to the child?

>Jerry V: I saw someone take the kid out of the house. An older woman got him and escorted him out of the house. I think she helped him pack a suitcase. I don't know if the woman was a relative or a social worker from DHS.

>*2 more comments*

Crissy T: I did a little asking around at City Hall and found out the diveway guy's kid did get taken to DHS that night. He's in a foster home now. They haven't made a determination about where he's going next.

>Jerry V: I haven't seen the driveway guy since the police came. So the driveway kid can't go back home. That's so sad.

>Sondra E: It is sad.

>Lynn D: Serves him right.

>James D: **Lynn D** That's messed up. Did you call the cops on him? Did you call the police?

>Lynn D: I have rights. I didn't do anything you wouldn't do. This is my neighborhood too. I have kids. I have to protect my family.

>Jerry V: What an awful thing to do, **Lynn D**. He's just a guy who likes to sit in his driveway. How would you like it if someone took your kids away?

>Lynn D: No one is going to take my kids away. I'm a law abiding American. I don't do drugs.

>Jerry V: NO ONE EVER SAID HE DID DRUGS! YOU'RE JUST MAKING STUFF UP!!!

>Lynn D: Don't yell at me!

>Jerry V: Quit calling the cops on innocent people.

>*55 more comments*

Darrin D: I have learned that my wife, **Lynn D**, who is a dues-paying, law-abiding member of GoodNeighbor.com™ and the Blue Oak HOA, is being harassed on this app. People are yelling at her for protecting our property and our property values. Please cease and consist or I will have my lawyer contact you. Signed, Darrin Daws, Citizen.

>Jerry V: Hahahahahaha!

>James D: Signed it!? You signed it!? Well, I guess that makes it official.

>Jim J: Cease and consist? HAHAHAHAHAHA!!!

>Alex C: We are citizens too, **Darrin D**. And we are allowed to say what we want. No one is hurting anyone. We're simply expressing our opinions. It's our first amendment right!

>Lynn D: Maybe I'll express my second amendment rights.

>Jim J: **Lynn D** that's SO MESSED UP! Are you seriously threatening people with firearms? Are you going to stand outside your house with a gun?

>Darrin D: **Jim J** I am fully within my constitutional rights to do so.

>*123 more comments*

Sara C: I just wanted everyone to know my husband and I are quitting this app. Goodneighbor.com™ has been a great help to us, especially when we first moved in, but the atmosphere has just become too toxic. Everyone is arguing. It's too much.

>Todd G: Good for you **Sara C**! This place has become too political.

>James K: I agree completely.

>Lynn D: Political? Is that a crack about our flags out front? I see you pointing at our flags **Todd G** while you laugh at us with your wife. Just go ahead and keep listening to NPR and having your little back yard parties with your friends.
>*14 more comments*

Crissy T: That guy who hangs out in the driveway came back home last night.
>Jim J: Was his kid with him?
>Crissy T: No.
>*2 more comments*

Crissy T: Another update on the man you call Driveway Guy. He was out in the driveway all night. His kid wasn't at the screen door, because he's with a foster family. But Driveway Guy was out all night in the driveway. With his chalk. He was drawing. Consulting that little notebook he has. Drew this gigantic circular design, it covered every inch of the driveway. And it wasn't like the last one, which was sort of pretty, this decoration that looked like a maze. The one he drew last night looked different. It was all sharp angles. Like teeth and claws, knives and swords. It was scary.
>Jim J: Poor guy. I hope he hasn't lost it.
>*3 more comments*

James D: The police were called and an investigation begun over the horribly mutilated animals fond at the bottom of the dumpsters last week. Trust me, the perpetrators will be found. Until that time, we are beginning the HOA dumpster program again, with some changes. There will only be one dumpster, in the vacant lot just off Carroll and Logan. The hours of dumpster use are limited to 10 a.m. to 4 p.m. A volunteer will be posted at the dumpster during those hours, and we will be checking I.D.'s to ensure everyone who uses the dumpster is from the Blue Oaks subdivision. Thank you for your cooperation. If you live in Blue Oak, the police may be knocking on your door for more information.
>Jim J: The dumpster is going to be guarded? And our I.D.'s are going to be checked? AND the police will be visiting all of us? I don't think so. I'd rather pay $50 to take my stuff down to the dump and get rid of it myself.

>Jerry C: Thank you for going to all this trouble set up the dumpsters for the HOA again. I know what hard work it is. I, for one, appreciate the added safety of knowing the dumpsters are monitored and identification is being checked.
>*1 more comment*

Jerry V: Driveway Guy flipped out this afternoon. The woman who left with his kid the night the police came came back. With his kid. She's from DHS I think. They both walked into the house together. They were there for about three hours.
>Jim J: Does he get to keep his kid?
Jerry V: I don't know. I heard some arguing coming from the house. And for sound to travel across the street it needs to be loud. When the front door opened the DHS lady and the kid came out. The kid was going along willingly.
>Jim J: What did Driveway Guy do?
>Jerry V: He screamed at them as they walked to the driveway and got into the car. About how they didn't have the right to take him away. About how he would get his revenge on those who took his child from him. About how he was going to make death rain down from the sky. It was really pretty freaky.
>Jim J: Maybe he is crazy.
>James D: I know I'd be crazy if someone took my kids away.
>Jerry V: He pointed at the drawing on his driveway. Said it was the last thing she's ever see. His voice sounded scary.
>James D: The last thing she'd ever see? That's pretty intense.
>Todd G: Don't do anything illegal and no one will take your kids away.
>Jerry V: He didn't do anything illegal!
>Lynn D: Serves him right.
>*15 more comments*

Jerry V: Some crazy lady went up and rang Driveway Guy's doorbell this afternoon. I don't know who it was, though I think it was someone in the neighborhood, because she walked up to the door. She didn't have a car. They argued in the doorway awhile. When she walked away, he followed her, like he did with the police. Same stuff too, about revenge, about fire and blood. He kept looking up and pointing as he talked.

>Jim J: Poor guy. The stress of the whole thing must have driven him crazy. I hope things get better.

>Jerry V: The kid left with the lady. I doubt things are going to get better.

>Todd G: Maybe she's protecting the kid. Maybe she's just doing her job. Why is she automatically the bad guy? The guy's a druggie, and he sounds pretty crazy too.

>Jerry V: **Todd G**, none of that is true and you know it. He's not a druggie and he's not crazy. You and **Lynn D** are spreading rumors.

>Jim J: Do you know if he's fighting to get the kid back?

>Jerry V: I'm sure he is. He was pretty upset.

>Darrin D: **Jerry V** please stop making baseless accusation concerning my wife.

>Jerry V: Serves her right!

>*5 more comments*

Susan P: I saw a bunch of police out last night about a block way. Not in front of the Driveway Guy's house, quite a few doors down. I think it was about a missing kid.

>Alyx C: I saw them out too. The woman who lives there—she's on the GoodNeighbor.com™ app but I don't want to invade her privacy— was screaming and crying. At first I thought it was a murder. I still think it must have been a gruesome death of some kind. Because her reaction was so intense. But no ambulance ever came. No dead body got taken away.

>Sondra E: So sorry. Such a sad world. I hope she's okay.

>*1 more comments*

Susan P: More police last night. Two nights in a row. Last night was a rerun of the night before. Several police cars came, a woman was crying and screaming at the door like there was a death or something, but no ambulance, and no body.

>Alyx C: I watched a little more carefully this time. I could overhear a little of what they were saying. Her kid is missing. He was playing in the back yard, and he didn't come in for lunch, and when mom went to check on him he was gone. The back yard was just empty. He's always supposed to check in before he leaves the house. He's never done anything like this before.

>Todd G: He's on drugs.

>Jim J: You're on drugs.

>Jerry V: Good Lord, he's not on drugs, **Todd G**. If he was on drugs, it might help.

>*14 more comments*

Lynn D: I know it's been mentioned on here before. And I know all of you on GoodNeighbor.com™ hate me. But my little boy is missing. He was playing in the back yard last Saturday. I was inside. I looked out the window and he was gone. He's never done this before. Never even left the yard until now. Please, if any of you saw him, or think you saw him, reach out to us with a DM. We are so worried.

>Sara C: Our thoughts and prayers are with you.

>Lynn D: Thank you.

>Darrin D: Thank you.

>Jerry V: **Sara C** I thought you quit this app.

>*125 more comments*

Cloe S: OMG! My kid came into the kitchen crying so hard he was barely able to talk. He just cried and pointed up into the sky, keeping his eyes closed. I went out there and I know this sounds crazy but some big and dark was disappearing into the sky. I thought it was a UFO at first, but I swear to God it had wings, and was flapping them. The wind from the wings knocked over the swing set!

>Jim J: Look who's on drugs now.

>Lynn D: That's an awful thing to say. Our kids are in danger and you are making fun of us? I'm sure it's so easy to sit there and do your drugs and text on your phone and listen to rap music and judge all of who aren't quite as hip as you are.

>Cloe S: It's okay, **Lynn D**, I don't mind. Anyway. Be careful! Look up! I didn't realize until today I almost never look up.

>*15 more comments*

Jerry V: Driveway guy totally lost it last night. Like, LOST it. He left the driveway, he was out in the yard, jumping around, like he was dancing, acting all crazy. He was screaming, shaking his fists at the sky. I didn't see anything up there. I looked. Believe me, after reading the last couple of posts on Goodneighbor, I made sure and looked up. Nothing.

>Jim J: The pressure must have broke him. That bitch down the street who called the cops and DHS, she broke him.

>Jerry V: The blood's on her hands.

>Earnest T: Jerry V, don't you think you're being a little overly dramatic?

>Darrin D: I have reported this thread to Goodneighbor.com™. Your use of gratuitous profanity and your continued insults against my wife violate the terms of service of Goodnighbor.com™. I know several people who have left the app because of your juvenile antics.
****THIS POST HAS VIOLATED OUR TERMS OF SERVICE AND HAS BEEN FROZEN. FURTHER VIOLATIONS WILL RESULT IN EXPULSION.
WELCOME TO THE NEIGHBORHOOD!
GOODNEIGHBOR.COM****

James D: After initial delays, the dumpster project was a complete success. We hauled off six dumpster-loads of trash to the city dump so far, and donated toys and food to several non-profits in the local area. Thank you to the entire Blue Oaks subdivision, and to the Blue Oaks HOA, for making this such a success. One more weekend and the dumpsters will be gone.

>Jerry C: **James D** more than glad to help. Thank you for leading the HOA!

>Doug R: Thank you for allowing us to clean out our garage!

>Sue T: Yes, what Doug said, I don't know what we'd do without the annual dumpsters. It'd cost a fortune to haul all this stuff to the dump.

>Diana C: I don't know if I'd call a dumpster filled with maimed and murdered neighborhood pets is what I'd call a complete success, but I get your drift. Thanks for helping.

>*3 more comments*

Earnest T: That movie I was talking about, about the giant dragon that lived in the buildings high above the city, it had a moral. I guess two morals, if you count the one about never looking up. But the other moral was, if you piss off a monster, it kills everyone. It doesn't care if you are good or evil. I think in the movie they messed with the lizard's egg. And it went crazy and killed everyone as revenge for messing with the egg.

>Jim J: Like Frankenstein. Or Godzilla. They only attack because they were provoked.

>Jerry V: You can't blame the destruction of Tokyo on Godzilla.

>Alyx C: I'm pretty sure you can, actually.

>Earnest T: Well, regardless, the moral of the story stands. Piss off a monster and everybody dies.

>*1 more comments*

Susan P: Another missing kid! Just down the block. The police came just like they did the other two times. I got more information this time, I went out and talked to the cops. I talked to the next door neighbor too. FIVE KIDS are missing from our neighborhood. Runaways, mostly, is what the cops say. The families don't say that at all. They say the kids were not the runaway type. They say the kids just disappeared. From back yards, from playgrounds. One of the kids disappeared while he was walking home from school. They were all outside when they disappeared. No one saw anything. I think we are dealing with a ring of pedophiles. The police, of course, said that was ridiculous.

>Jerry V: The police are just trying to find a way to not do their jobs.

>Alyx C: What's wrong with you all? Can't you see what's happening? IT'S THE DRIVEWAY GUY! He's exacting his revenge! He's taking our children! He's punishing us!

>Jim J: I'm sorry, **Alyx C**, I'm a pretty open-minded guy, but that just seems crazy. The kids are just runaways, I'm sure. No pedophiles. No sky monsters swooping out of the sky to snatch them up.

>Jerry V: She's smoking whatever driveway guy is smoking.

>*72 more comments*

Lynn D: HE'S TAKING THE CHILDREN! CAN'T YOU SEE THE TRUTH!? HE'S STEALING OUR CHILDREN! That crazy old man is taking his revenge on me! He's taking his revenge on us all!

>Jim J: Calm down, Karen.

>Lynn D: LOOK UP! CAN'T EVERYBODY JUST LOOK UP AND SEE THE TRUTH?

>Chrissy T: I'm sorry, dear, you seem very frustrated. I understand, and when a child goes missing the whole world seems to turn against you. Is there someone you can talk to? Do you have a therapist?

>Jim S: I agree. Lynn D, our thoughts and prayers are with you as you go through this difficult time.
>*232 more comments*

Jim J: OMG I just saw it! I just saw some bird-lizard thing come down and snatch up a kid! Like, right across the street! I was out on the porch smoking and saw the whole thing happen. I dropped my pipe! This kid, Zane, he was out in the front yard, really early in the morning. I had just come home from work. I could see his Mom making breakfast in the kitchen. And then this dark thing came down, it was so fast, I didn't really see the color, just DARK, and he just grabbed the kid with these horrible clawed feet and then they were both just gone. I looked up and nothing. Maybe a dot disappearing into the clouds. The whole thing was over in 10 seconds.
>Lynn D: I told you.
>Darrin D: Serves him right.
>Jim J: Serves who right, **Darrin D**? He's a little kid. He didn't hurt anyone. He's innocent.
>Earnest T: Remember what I said. Piss off a monster and everyone dies.
>Jim J: Yeah, but who's the monster?
>Earnest T: Just make sure and keep looking up. These are strange times.
>*15 more comments*

Jerry C: There's cops swarming around the dumpsters! Does anyone know what's going on? They've blocked off the streets near there. There's five ambulances, and I don't know how many police cars. Nobody's talking. You can't even call people in those houses, all you get is a busy signal. All the houses.
>Jim K: **James D** , do you know what's going on?
>Denise P: Something is smeared all over the side of the dumpster. And the fence next to it. Is it oil? Motor oil?
>Jim S: Holy shit! Is that blood? I swear that looks like blood.
>James D: The police is taking samples. I don't think that's motor oil.
>Lynn D: It's BLOOD.
>*523 more comments*

Sara S: There's news vans everywhere too. My phone's ringing off the hook. Texts, emails. What's going on? Does anyone know what's going on?

>Doug R: We're on TV. Channel 6. Tune in.

>Jim J: TV? Channel 6? Dude, we're all over the internet! We're national news! Worldwide news!

>Sara S: Is anyone saying what's going on?

>3277 more comments

Jim J: Help. I'm hiding in the corner of my porch. One of those things is out in the street. I called the police, but they thought I was high. And I am high, but that doesn't mean it's not there. So, I'm posting here, because I know at least a few of the people here will believe me.

>Jerry V: Hey, you okay, man?

>Jim J: I dropped my phone and I had to go out on the lawn to get it. Now I can't get to my front door. It's staring at me. It knows I'm here. I think it senses motion.

>Jerry V: Did you call 911?

>Jim J: YES! They didn't believe me.

>Jerry V: Buddy, you know I'm cool with the weed thing, but could it be you smoked a little too much?

>Jim J: It's got this thing on its head. This design. In circle, Sharps knives and teeth and claws and blood. An eye in the center. It's scary AF.

>Jerry V: OMG Hang in there buddy.

>Jim J: You know what the design means?

>Jerry V: Driveway Guy mentioned it. He drew it on his driveway, remember? He told the DHS lady it'd be the last thing she ever saw.

>Jerry V: Jim? Jim, are you there? Should I call 911.

>Jim J: I dropped my phone. It saw me I think. Shit, it's coming closer. I'm going to make a run for the door.

>Sara S: I'm on the block too. Is this happening right now?

>Jerry V: **Jim J** NO! Let me call 911.

>Jim J: 911 doesn't care. 911 is already here, out at the dumpster. I'm going. Wish me luck.

>Jerry V: Wait, hold on, I think I actually see you! Are you pressed against the stairs?

>Jim J: Yes!

>Jerry V: Wait. There's a garden gnome right next to you? And a home security sign?

>Jim J: YES! THAT'S ME! I'm going to try to get up the stairs an into the house before he can get to me.

>Jerry V: NO! WAIT! Not yet! He's too close! Here, let me help. I'll run out in the street and get its attention.

>Sara S: I see you too! OMG I see it! Don't go! Please don't move! It looks like it's ready to pounce!

>Jerry V: Don't risk your life. Stay hidden. I'm going out into the street and get his attention, then run inside! Wait on me!

Sara S: **Jim J! Jerry V!** Don't go!

Jim J: Okay. I'm ready. Wish me luck! Here I go!

Jerry V: I'm going too! Wait on me.

Sara S: NO!!! **Jim J! Jerry V!** Don't go! Are either of you still there? Hello? I'm so scared. Please don't move.

Sara S: Hello? **Jim J? Jerry V?**

>*12,217 more comments*

THIS THREAD HAS BEEN FROZEN BY LAW ENFORCEMENT. PLEASE CONSULT GOODNEIGHBOR.COM™ TERMS OF SERVICE FOR AN EXPLANATION OF LIMITATIONS OF LIABILITY. WELCOME TO THE NEIGHBORHOOD!

Jeff Wood lives in Colorado, where he spends way too much time staring at the night sky, and a little too much time watching baseball. His stories have appeared in over 40 publications such as Amazing Monster Tales, Boston Phoenix, New York Press, Wild Musette, Fiction at Work, Bright Desire, The Greyrock Review, Bellowing Ark, *and* Java Journal. *He has a children's play included in the anthology* Childsplay, *in the company of such authors as Sam Shepard and Maya Angelou.*

SOMETHING SINISTER IS HIDING IN THE SMALL TOWN OF PERCY, INDIANA...
TOUCH THE NIGHT
MAX BOOTH III

"A cult classic
waiting on its cult."
-William Boyle

SHE
WAS
FOUND
IN A
GUITAR
CASE

DAVID JAMES KEATON

"The universes David James Keaton creates have one foot in stark reality
and the other in the oneiric realm of barroom stories and urban legends."
-Dead End Follies

And now, an exclusive excerpt of *She Was Found in a Guitar Case* by David James Keaton, now available from Perpetual Motion Machine

I

MY WIFE WAS FOUND IN A GUITAR CASE

WHILE I WAS still trying to figure out what to do with the mystery animal I'd rescued from the dumpster, cops were working my door like a speed bag, eager as hell to tell me my wife had been found dead in a guitar case. I opened up to stop the pounding and found three righteous knuckleheads perched on my porch, rocking back and forth on their shoes. One big, one small, with a medium-sized buzzcut standing in the middle. The two bookends were bright blue, wringing the hats in their hands real noble, while the middle guy was the porridge that was just "white" apparently, wearing the sharp suit, bright shirt with a starched collar, and a blood-red power tie that divided him neatly in half. He was clearly in charge. He looked me up, down, up, right, down, left, up, head twitching like a thumb memorizing a videogame cheat code. Because of this grim trifecta of foreheads furrowed like fists, as well as the rest of the insufferably officious body language being thrown at me, I knew immediately they'd come to report something horrible. Even though Angie hadn't been missing long enough for me to be fully prepared for the absolute worst, I'd actually watched a movie or two in my life and knew this scene well. So, in that moment, my certainty that these three police officers were going to be comforted later by loved ones dutifully impressed with their noble task of delivering tragic news to idiots such as myself had eclipsed any shock to become my focus.

In the five seconds it took them to square up and give me the *Always Sunny* ocular pat-down, I'd already imagined a decade of their dinner-table conversations, and I was thoroughly convinced they got off on these sorts of assignments. It might be difficult being some guy dealing with a murdered wife, but holy hell, how about the poor souls who have to inform distraught civilians about their spouse, child, or dog shattered on the highway? I pictured the cops making sure their wives caught them staring pensively at the horizon, or into their shaving mirrors, a silent countdown to a sympathetic back rub or blowjob. Okay, sure, I figured their training meant these guys were reasonably interested in my reaction, too. But only if it was a reasonable one. And it never was.

Suspense was emulating from them, almost like an audible hum (though this might have been coming from a walkie-talkie). I knew from my previous job closed-captioning a thousand true-crime shows that I, as the husband in the equation, was no doubt the prime suspect. They were watching for me to fuck up. And the detective in the middle, with his bottom-of-the-barrel semiotic strategies of interrogation (red power tie pointing at his groin, for example) had this objective written all over his scowl, causing what could have been an innocuous encounter to be blighted by expectation. Blame them, not me.

So, in spite of my confidence clocking their motivations at 99% accuracy (at least), and my very real horror at the prospect of losing the love of my life, none of this mental chess stopped me from being the most suspicious man in the history of bad news delivered on doorsteps. I could feel the misdirected rage boiling up and over and ricocheting in all the wrong directions before I could stop it, even if I'd wanted to.

"Mr. James . . ." the small cop began. "We're sorry to inform you that . . . "

Somewhere in the rumble of blood in my ears, I heard the words "wife," "murdered," and "guitar" rolling off the hot breath of this dude, and I had questions. But I couldn't stop thinking how they were relishing their roles as harbingers of doom. What kind of person does this nature of work? And who needs three of them to do it?

I was really stuck on all this.

Mainly because I knew they were watching me experience something I'd always found excruciating to witness in others: when tragedy becomes an excuse to be a monster. And if there were two things that captioning true crime and the occasional shitkicker Bigfoot hunting show had taught me, it was that monsters were ridiculous. And that a guitar-and-banjo duel could break out at any moment. Also, human beings didn't fit in guitar cases. Okay, that's three things.

But since we have a little time right now with my eyes closed and the thunder of my eardrums obscuring the scene on the porch, let's rewind to my first memory of the bad-reaction loophole I'd been cursed with forever. It goes back further but involves much lower stakes. In high school when I delivered pizzas, a co-worker got the mirror knocked off her car by some bump-and-run, and she came running into the shop yelling, "Call the cops, dummies!" But I hesitated, understandably wanting details, and she flipped out, upending the perfectly symmetrical pizza I was crafting, screaming inches from my nose. I remember thinking, "No *way* you're this upset. You just wanted to trash my pizza 'cause we broke up." See, I understood the urge to hurl a pre-cooked floppy disc of pizza dough across the room to see how it landed. And I understood that, in such a moment, you are hovering in a limbo of split-second understanding that you're going to take advantage of your newfound, tragedy-induced immunity in case the opportunity never arises again. But what I didn't understand was . . . you are also genuinely upset. So there on my doorstep, I finally appreciated why she'd launched my first geometrically perfect pie into a ceiling fan, and I opened my eyes and rubbed my ears red and ground my teeth in a vibrating crimson haze of despair that was still coherent enough to hope these cops gave me any reason at all to flip their metaphorical pizzas right the fuck out.

Later, I got more facts about the case, the horrible stuff, about how she likely survived in that guitar case for almost half a day, hogtied and folded up and running out of life while she listened to truck after truck piling the city's trash over her. But in that moment at the front door staring at this real-life representation of an Ascent of Man evolution poster, I just really wanted to hurt these guys. Future blowjobs be damned.

I scanned the big one, with his all-too-enthusiastic hat wringing, his lumpy blue shirt making his matching necktie practically invisible and therefore powerless, and I imagined him using these encounters to explain away impotence, alcoholism, maybe missing his lumpen, mouth-breathing spawn's big moment of sanctioned assault in a hockey game, probably when he hip-checked the first female player in the history of their school headfirst into the boards.

"When did this happen?" I asked, watching his mouth wriggling around so much that it practically ate itself, and now I was utterly convinced he'd definitely conceived a shitty, hockey-playing kid. I squeezed my doorjamb and watched my own knuckles turn as white as his face. I was extra strong in doorjambs, you see. Even though I hadn't gotten to the point where I could do 500 chin-ups on the bar I'd hung in our sagging bedroom-door frame, today I was squeezing this wood so hard all three of them heard the cracking. Though I couldn't be sure this wasn't just my knuckles.

"Well, sir, we don't know much," the detective in the middle answered, holding up a hand to keep Lumpy quiet. "But due to blood pooling in her right arm and leg, as well as the necrotic tissue frozen to the hinges of the guitar case, we believe, at this time, she was killed in another location, possibly struck by an automobile, and, subsequently, brought to the garbage dump."

"No shit," I said, not really asking, not really talking, just squeezing the door harder despite the cramps. "So, you're saying she didn't live there? At the garbage dump, I mean. So you're saying you got cutting-edge forensics telling you her day didn't start on a mountain of crushed beer cans and loaded diapers and gutted TV dinners? Thanks, supersleuth!"

"I'm sorry, sir, we're still trying to ascertain . . ."

"*'Ascertain'*? How about you stop trying to sound like some rent-a-cop on the witness stand bumbling over big words and just tell me what you know about my wife."

"We understand that you're upset." The little one stepped forward, screwing his hat back on his pointed head to exert some authority. "And you have our word, Mr. James, that we will do everything in our power to . . ."

"Now, can you tell us . . . " Lumpy started to say over him, and at that I stepped completely out of my house and into their arena, eyeball to eyeball with the disheveled one now, and, oh shit, he didn't like me in his bubble at all. But I figured I wouldn't get another chance like this, to toss their perfect pizza into the fan blades, so I stepped even closer. Today was my diplomatic immunity, before my depression or their defensiveness took over. I'd always wanted to get pulled over speeding when my wife was going into labor. They'd say, "Follow us!" and put on the sirens, and we'd all break the laws together, pizzas flying everywhere. All of us trapped together in this bubble, impervious in a shield of rising crust. And dangling heavy on the vine of a bending skyline, a nuclear explosion of tomato-red goodness.

"Listen, please don't use the word 'power' when you stand there twisting the sweat out of your lid," I said, right up his nose. I considered a quick bite on the booze-busted blood vessels at the end of his beak, but I kept it together. "You stand there fantasizing how you can tell this story over pork chops to your halfwit family of hockey players, and still I have to endure making you feel okay about making me feel bad?" What's weird is I loved hockey.

The big one blinked at this, getting a little fire back in his face, remembering I was just some citizen disrespecting him, and he went for his mirror glasses to push back with some steely-eyed sovereignty. But a hand appeared on his shoulder, then his hand appeared on that guy's shoulder, then on my own shoulder, then a couple more hands clapped over each other's chests, and miraculously this impromptu game of Twister calmed everyone back down. I looked around and started counting this weirdly comforting *Human Centipede* of cupped hands and wedding rings, and now it was impossible to blow up.

One, two, three, four, five, six, seven . . . wait, how many paws do these guys got?

"Sir, we know how upsetting this must be. But be assured, because of her pregnancy, we, as a result, now have ourselves, at this point, another homicide case to pursue."

"How did you know she was six weeks pregnant? I thought autopsies took days."

"This case is a priority," one of them said, mouth not moving.

"Okay, let me ask you a question," I said, then tried out a small shove against the big guy's chest. He stumbled down a step, and the other two held up their hands.

"Whoa, whoa . . ."

"Okay, two questions," I said. "When you guys run your mouths, how much do all those commas cost? More than bullets?"

"What?"

"Do you think I'm stupid? Do you think *I think* they really scrambled some special fetus squad instead of the usual team of incompetents? Maybe I'll follow you so I can watch you guys knock on five more doors and look sincere while you twist and fumble with your goddamn invisible ties. Or maybe we can just jump ahead to the TV screen that will read 'Ten Years Later,' because stay tuned, *maybe* you catch a break and finally catch a killer. Doubt it, though."

Hands were back on everybody's shoulders but mine.

"Let's go, Joe," the small one said, pulling the lumpy one away. I watched them get into their car, the detective looking like he still had a lot to say to me. So I pushed my luck and trailed them to the cruiser, knocking on the window good and hard. I'd always wanted to do that, too. The detective stood with his door open, and the big lumpy cop, the driver, rolled down his window, cheeks puffed in frustration as he held his breath behind pursed lips.

That's when I saw their hands hadn't been clapping each other's chests and shoulders to restrain themselves after all. They'd been covering up the electronic eyes of their body cameras, in case one of them snapped along with me.

A brave new world, I decided. *And a whole new type of restraint.*

"One last question," I said. "Have you heard of the Flynn Effect?"

He looked at his partner. Of course he hadn't.

"It was something my wife was working on," I explained. "Something from her doctoral research. It means every generation is smarter than the previous one. And it means our generation cannot think in the hypothetical. My unborn child might have been able to do this, but we have no chance. And one thing I now understand is I'll forever be unable to consider such hypothetical situations."

The big one shook his head at all this shit and started the car.

"Don't leave town, Mr. James," the detective said finally, pausing for effect as he climbed in. "Someone will be by to talk to you again soon."

I smiled. Even though I'd just found out my wife was dead and I was now beginning the second half of my cursed life where everything that made sense for half a minute when we were together and happy would no longer be recognizable and my previous life was just some bad movie we saw once where we had no interest in the ending. I smiled mostly because I could do something in that moment to make a cop feel foolish. And how often do you get the chance? The smile would cost me months of guilt and incrimination, and, eventually, something even worse, but it was probably worth it.

"Are you actually telling me you can't imagine anyone not thinking in the hypothetical!" I yelled like a fool as they drove off.

They didn't get the joke, and I may have laughed. Angie would have laughed. But laughing is something you don't do after cops tell you your wife was found dead in a guitar case. Something you definitely don't do if your wife died carrying your child. But lost innocence and laughing at cops was a combination as natural as chocolate and peanut butter, and, more importantly, there was no way I would let them record me crying.

But I didn't have to worry. They were gone, and any dashboard cameras or body cameras or covert plastic eyeballs would miss any honest reaction, even if it was no different from a manufactured one, or if I had no idea what that has ever looked like.

***

After the cops left, I may have stood there for an extra dozen deep breaths, even considered sticking around if I had any faith in the Louisville Police Department, or if I hadn't so effectively gotten the investigation off on the wrong foot by jamming mine in my mouth. And my feet continued to screw me up, as I stumbled around trying to figure out why my jeans suddenly didn't seem to have any leg holes, and I thought about my wife and our future baby curled up in a guitar case like grisly Russian nesting dolls. I thought about how much she would have enjoyed that doorway exchange, considering her recent anti-authoritarian research for her dissertation, but mostly I kicked at my elusive pant legs and thought about how we'd always joked about her height, about her being so short a hawk might swoop down to grab her on a jog. Which is kinda what happened after all. But she was no nesting doll. It just didn't make any sense. A guitar case? Even Angie wasn't that small.

"Matryoshkas," she told me once. "That's what those dolls were called." I'd mangled the word when we came across a pile of discarded playground hobby horses during our trip to France, stacked up high under an overpass and rusting away in order of decreasing size. She loved horses, even metal ones, even though she knew this was "expected of females."

I thought about how impossibly small a guitar case was, how there was no way to comfortably house a human body, alive or dead. I remembered the time we'd watched instrument cases playing musical chairs and chasing each other around a Louisville airport carousel, after Paris, as we stood waiting for our lost luggage. We were getting frustrated by the passengers breathing down our necks and elbowing us in the ribs, all waiting for missing bags, too. We got a good laugh when one stubby leather fiddle case got stuck on the conveyor belt and backed up the bags to upset everyone even more, until a guitar case finally slid down to knock it loose. It was brown, an artificial wood laminate, but covered in stickers of every kind of flower, mostly daisies? No, orange blossoms. I almost grabbed it, maybe to pull the guitar out of it and pretend it was mine as an excuse to abandon our stuff and be done with that long travel day. I told Angie about my plan, and she asked me, "What if you had to prove you could play it?"

But there was a padlock on the guitar case, thank Christ, so it was back to waiting. She was always three steps ahead of my bad ideas, and we stood there for two more hours, watching suitcases and boxes and musical instruments slide down the chute and around our sad cul-de-sac for at least four more flights before we found out from a sleepwalking employee that our luggage was safely on its way to Chicago, three hundred miles away. But while we waited for that surprise to ruin our mood completely, we relived our Paris trip there in the airport, laughing through the highlights. And France was good for us, too, even while it was happening, which was rare. It rekindled things for a bit, as a trip to Paris is mandated by the United Nations to do, but our trip also benefited from her previous knowledge of the city. She'd been there for a conference on "composition and rhetoric," two things I knew little about (though I followed her blindly into a teaching career of my own). She'd already mapped out all the best places she missed the first time, so while I thought of the trip as a marriage life preserver, she thought of it in terms of "maximum efficiency." Either way, I told myself we both considered this trip a second chance to get something right.

But she really did map it out within an inch of its life, like a surgeon drawing dotted lines all across our bodies to get ready for the knife. We launched our tour at the heart, a.k.a. the Sacre Coeur, then the Eiffel Tower, of course, then next we hit those terrifying Catacombs beneath the streets and the millions of bones housed within, then the French Museum of Natural History and its notoriously chilling "spider cats"-in-jars exhibit. And finally, the Ugly American Abroad timeless tradition ... we proudly clamped a "love lock" onto the Passerelle des Arts bridge.

We didn't have a real passion for that last adventure, actually, at least until a thinkpiece on NPR and an essay in *The New Yinzer* shamed Americans for doing this. Then Angie was all about it. "French love locks are vandalism!" the articles screamed. "Ancient architecture is being destroyed!" This got us curious enough to smuggle some padlocks into the country, like we were getting away with something. "Fuck the Patriot

Act," Angie told the guy at the hardware store, flirting like she did, and she ended up buying a lock featured on commercials showcasing its resistance to a spectacular fireworks display of repeated, close-range shotgun blasts. Angie bought a ton of locks actually, since there was a sale and she loved to "get the deal." I still had a whole drawer of the suckers, which would remain forever unlocked. She put heart stickers on all their stubby keys and drew American flags on all their steel flanks, mostly because it was the most obnoxious "Freedom Fries" thing we could think of. Well, we tried to anyway. Not a whole lot of room on a padlock for artistry or identifiable flags, even if they do soak up gunfire real good. Just keep in mind that, when we vandalized famous bridges, my wife would spend three times the money so the locals couldn't scam us. And once we got to the Passerelle des Arts, we already had a variety of new theories about the recent online outrage to chew on:

First, we figured the internet scolds were probably just bitter because they didn't think ahead to smuggle a padlock into the country, and maybe he/she got ripped off by some local charging 50 euro for one, which was something like 947 American dollars and wonderful for the French economy. Or maybe the article was written by a bona fide "he/she," and the author could hold hands with itself and had no one to impress, let alone lock down. In any case, we were vindicated when, once on the bridge, we saw that 90% of the dewy-eyed lovers who were attaching these locks and snapping pictures after the fact were French as fuck. We knew this because, when they asked us to take their picture, we heard their unmistakable but adorably problematic Pepé Le Pew accents. Most Americans at least have the self-respect to selfie that shit and not ask for assistance.

"Gather 'round for some history!" Angie explained to whoever would listen. "Did you know this lock-bridge tradition is featured in the movie *Amélie*, an adorable whimsy-fest *and* the French equivalent of getting an endorsement by Uncle Sam herself? Of course you did. Because this movie was clearly what inspired you French to go nuts on these bridges. And now you're mad when the rest of the world takes you up on it? Case dismissed!"

Trivia note: the love-lock thing was also featured on an episode of *Parks and Recreation*, one of Angie's favorite shows, so she figured there was no way Leslie Knope didn't consider any and all negative implications.

She was all about this ritual for historic reasons, too. According to legend, her mom and dad had done this love-lock action, back on their own honeymoon. Or maybe it was her grandpa. Definitely not the brother, as he died young (speaking of locks, he was dumb enough to work in a prison and realized his poor choice of vocation way too late). But whoever it was, it was real important to someone in her family that we do this, and someone had called Angie when we were overseas and she got real serious about us getting it done. Come to think of it, her dad even had a job in the factory making the damn things. Or maybe it was prison. But despite the way Angie described it—like we were just being the Obstinate Americans—it was actually kind of a religious ritual for her family, though none of them were religious at all (at least as far as I knew). But I guess it could have been one of those new wacky religions, where you had no choice, or one of those *old* wacky ones, where you had no recollection.

We forgot to throw our keys in the river and finish her ceremony, though. Something distracted us, probably some French asshole trying to sell us ten more padlocks. It wasn't that I didn't want to litter in that river. Hell, I would have kicked a taxi's side mirror into the water for her if I could, because my love was a *beast* back then. But I just stuck the key back on my toy camera keychain—a gesture that at least one local scammer told me was bad luck for any relationship.

Proved him wrong today, huh?

Here's the thing, though, the real reason behind those internet haters and local swindlers: The parts of the bridge soaking up all our ugly tourist locks have never been ancient at all! Buncha spare parts, new materials, mostly replicas built back in the '80s, which makes romantic river walks only slightly more vintage than, say, a Sylvester Stallone movie, and with the same sag at the mouth.

"Who are they fucking kidding?" Angie said to our Parisian hotel concierge with the name I can't remember right now (but it was something so ridiculous you wouldn't believe me). "The panels with the locks? The 'ancient architecture' they talked about on NPR? Just a bunch of puke-green chain-link fence. The kind of fence you'd see at a Little League game. I ask you, Fabio, is there anything uglier than that? Remember those candy-coated fences from the 1800s? Yeah, me neither."

Our concierge who was totally named "Fabio" shook his head that day, but it was clear he knew she was right. And if that kind of hideous contemporary fence wasn't already catnip for attaching locks, then they'd probably have to put up the chain-link regardless, to stop love-struck locals from flinging themselves into the waves, which was infinitely dumber than throwing a key, right? Which I forgot to do. Throw the key or myself into the water, I mean.

But the point Angie was making was that padlocks looked way better than a rubbery split-pea barricade, and *my* point was she could talk any Frenchmen into siding with goddamn tourists, even Fabio. Just one of her skills.

So we stood there in the airport, watching nylon coffins crammed with tiny toiletries and even smaller plastic landmarks dance around the circle, while Angie got a little punch drunk, continuing to defend the tacky love-lock trend for anyone who was eavesdropping.

"You know, the Eiffel Tower is built with a lot of fence work and holes, so it looks pretty conducive to padlocks," she said, louder than necessary. "Coincidence? No way. The French love locks! A friend told me they dump off sections of fence to make room for more, so they're also job creators. Real talk? How hard would it be to make a lock-resistant bridge?"

"Who are you talking to?" I asked her, sighing. "I was there, remember?"

"You know, some of this same stuff about the locks I found in the Ohio archives while researching my dissertation. You'd know if you read it."

"I thought your dissertation was on prison."

"It's complicated, Dave. Cheap prison labor is on the rise, especially for tourist junk. And out there in the Midwest, they have copycat bridges. Did you know that padlock panels and sectors of fences, some from all over the world, end up in a huge warehouse in Ohio? Mark my words, Paris will start recycling their locks soon . . ."

"That sounds awesome actually. It's much more romantic to have your padlock get squirrelled away in a dark warehouse *Raiders of the Lost Ark*-style. We're so lucky we kept the key."

We weren't really fighting, at least I didn't think so. And I *did* think we were lucky, at least at the time. So, as we watched all the unclaimed luggage continue to do their laps, hoping for more odd-shaped instrument cases to break up the monotony, I thought about how society ached so hard for us to put a lock on that bridge, how any article trying to shame us, or any hand-wringing Parisian government types, were all merely reverse psychology geared towards our contrarian Westernized brains. Like they were saying, "We *dare* you to show your love . . ." There was such a pressure by the Gypsies on that bridge for us to lock something, somewhere, anywhere, that I thought they were going to pull a pin on a grenade if we didn't participate. Or maybe the pressure was just coming from Angie. Or her family. Later, I would discover it was all three.

Earlier, when we were still working our way through customs, we'd gotten the giggles and asked the TSA agent if we could get the "real" French passport stamp, the one with "the tiny cartoon padlock on it," and we were almost strip-searched on the spot. Angie had already downed about a gallon of wine on the flight, so we were still flying kinda high, and it was tough not to tell dour customs agents about the graffiti we'd seen on *actual human corpses* in the Catacombs under Paris. Oh, and all the illicit flash photography, which was no doubt blowing those bones to dust after a million skeleton-scorching photos a year. Real, live bones down there, not '80s replicas like those dumb bridges.

"Someone writing shit on skulls?" I whispered. "Now that's some real vandalism! And we got the skull selfies to prove it."

"Just keep the line moving, please, sir."

By the time we'd made it to the luggage carousel, we had stopped snickering, heads hanging low and the sleepy tail end of her wine buzz quieting us both down to some grumbles and teeth grinding. Then she pointed to a sign above our heads and laughed:

"Wouldn't it be more fun if that said 'Personal Baggage Claim' instead?"

It took me a second, but then I lost it, too, no matter how close to home that joke really was. I said to her, "Oh, you mean you'd rather watch a turnstile full of exes, neglectful parents, missed birthdays, broken promises, minor scandals, Electra and Oedipal complexes, all rolling down the ramp?"

"Yes. That," she declared. "Then these people might hesitate to swarm this carousel so damn close!"

It was officially the last thing she said on our honeymoon, then she snored through the Uber ride home. But everybody sure heard it. She always got away with stuff like that, maybe because of her height. And when she explained to me once how "Matryoshka" didn't really mean "nesting doll" at all, that it was just a name for little Russian biddies, any small but sturdy old lady, I realized this was her in a nutshell. Curled up in a nutshell, I mean, feet pinned over her head forever.

But that night at the airport, strangers backed up, clearing a path for her at the turnstile. She was small, but she had that kind of power.

***

Before I could come to my senses, I ran back inside our apartment and packed up all my stuff to leave town, jamming a couple soup-to-nuts changes of clothes into my suitcase. The Paris customs slips still dangled from the handle, and I thought about how a suitcase was almost too small to hold a reasonable stack of textile facsimiles of the average head-to-toe human being, let alone the entire thing, alive or otherwise.

And a guitar case was smaller than this? Insanity.

I patted my pockets and realized I'd lost my wallet somewhere in the chaos of the day, but a couple of my old driver's licenses were on the floor, so I gathered those up. I always saved my expired licenses, but the loss of my wallet and a valid I.D. (not to mention a visit from the goon squad), convinced me conclusively I was doing the right thing by getting the hell out of Dodge. Pulse pounding, I kicked my rubber horse head into the corner. It was a gift from Angie, but I was clear-headed enough to know there was only room for essentials.

But there was one final stop I needed to make.

I opened the bathroom door and stared for a good five minutes at the metal cage in the tub. The mystery creature was nosing the bars of its tiny prison.

Then I thought, "Fuck it," and gathered up my spirit animal and headed out.

***

The streets of Kentucky were quiet, even with my windows down, and I drove holding my breath in my throat. The DMV was right by our house, and I considered getting a new Kentucky license in spite of how strange that would seem after receiving news about a dead wife. This convinced me to do it.

But when I hit their lot, I saw it was the same spot I'd parked in the last time I'd lost my wallet, which was something that happened about twice a year. The same wizened old dude was smoking by the door, eyeballs clocking my car, and when I looked in my rearview, my beard was doing that same weird asymmetrical thing it did in my last license photo. It took me years to understand that this was simply because I drove with my head hanging out the window a little, like an animal. But this five-car pile-up of déjà vu changed my mind fast, and I pulled back out of the lot.

This is what a realistic Groundhog's Day *would look like*, I thought. *A straight-up horror movie with endless trips to the DMV. Nothing even close to a love story.*

I looked to the left and thought about Nashville, then to the right and thought about Ohio. Maybe I could stay with my dad in Toledo, tail between my legs. Ohio had its good qualities. And there must be plenty to do there, judging by how often Angie went back for research. Also in its favor was the fact that I couldn't remember seeing a single, solitary street musician staining the curbs or bridges of that state with their mediocre music . . .

Wait a second.

I steadied the cage in my passenger's seat and stomped the gas on my Rabbit, tearing ass down Bardstown road, back to the alley near the Keep Louisville Weird shop with the cut-out circus clown photo-op in front. This was the store where I used to make Angie laugh by trying on that same floppy rubber horse's head, but never buying it. It was always her idea to do it, and I would complain it would be terrible for a bank robbery because the eyes of the mask never lined up with my own, and she'd say, "Ride your horse for good, not evil."

It was funny enough, but I started to think it was a borderline fetish for her, because every Wednesday night, Angie and her girlfriends would head down to the Davis Arena for another Ohio Valley Wrestling Moron-O-Thon. The problem was Louisville's wrestling scene wasn't small enough for a bunch of smug PhD students to be there sarcastically, like Pittsburgh's ratty little Keystone State Wrestling Alliance had been when we'd hung out a couple times back in grad school. Her colleagues loved that nonsense, watching assholes munch light bulbs and press staplers and stick pins and thumbtacks into each other's heads. All the school supplies they could rustle up to press into each other's skulls with the ease of December porch pumpkins. But Davis Arena wasn't big enough to enjoy the full-on kitsch factor. Remember Arena Football? How embarrassing that shit was? Where it was kinda in the middle between NFL and college football? The porridge that was just stupid.

Angie's girlfriends would tease her because she'd root for this big dude who was supposedly "half stallion." I hoped they meant his head. Seriously though, there really was this Mexican kid who called himself the "Lucha Horse," rubber horse head and everything. I even bought her the T-shirt. At the time, she was addicted to one of those Learn Spanish apps, and I heard her chirping "cabello this" and "cabello that." I don't think this was a coincidence.

Goofy horse heads everywhere, though! It was a popular item in a big Derby town. And Keep Louisville Weird was where I'd chat up a clerk I called "'90s Ex-Girlfriend" because she had that reddish Kool-Aid flavored hair so popular back then. I'd have that clerk repeat how much the horse head cost at least a dozen times because all I could ever think about while looking at her was everything I wished I would have said to my real '90s ex-girlfriend who unceremoniously dumped me, like, "You're welcome for all the Meat Loaf mix tapes!" or "Sorry for all the orgasms!" or vice versa. They also had a terrifying life-size Walt Disney, who was sporting half a moustache and disintegrating faster than the real McCoy. But they had cool stuff, too, like Spencer's Gifts stuff (the O.G. Hot Topic), back before shopping malls morphed into boat shows. But the only thing I ever bought there was an ant farm, which you can get anywhere. Any chance I got (when I wasn't working through baggage with ex-girlfriends), I spent working through memories of the horror that befell my first ant farm back when I was a little kid. Thinking about that shit was my own Vietnam flashback. Or so I've heard from actual veterans. They ship those ants from Cambodia, you know?

"For prison research," Angie said, thumping it into my chest, and I was confused but didn't argue, not ready to breach the subject of the ant-farm tragedy from my past, now or then. I realize it seems ridiculous I can ponder the death of my wife easily enough, but not my misadventures in ants.

Now that I think about it, Keep Louisville Weird was also positively *infested* with musicians. So there I was, circling their stomping grounds, but the musicians were gone. Calling them "musicians" was probably a stretch. In any warm state, they were a common infection, a topical rash on any establishment. Where Angie had grown up in Minnesota, they called them "buskers," and this word made me homicidal the first time I heard it, way before I suspected one of murder.

So during my drive-by with my mystery pet and memories, I stopped outside the store, staring at a clean spot on the street where a guitar case used to be. At first glance, this spot resembled the curve of a woman's hips, and I could picture this particular guitar case on this particular corner because I was always amazed how little money the guy always made. I got out of the car and crouched down in the gutter to touch the edges of the sidewalk outline unmolested by the stain of dust and oil and dried rain, still unable to comprehend how my wife could have fit inside it. I glanced up at the store and thought about the horse head, and not just because I wished I was wearing it right now. Angie had wanted it to cap off our last Kentucky Derby costume before we moved. "The Jockey and Her Steed," she called it, and all she'd need was her '90s Fly Girl hat to complete the illusion. But what turned out to be our final Derby had been such a fiasco that the idea was dropped.

Inside, I could see '90s Ex-Girlfriend rearranging the skin-tight hipster Mothman T-shirts for the window display, and I noticed she was about six months pregnant, but only three months from the Kool-Aid flavor growing out of her hair completely.

Okay, I guess that makes her more like '80s Ex-Girlfriend, I thought, watching that belly swing and remembering my own misadventures with birth control, both then and now.

Then I heard the unmistakable sound of a musical instrument thrumming low inside its coffin, strings protesting as the case rebounded around off someone's scrawny knees, and I spun to see a musician slinking through the alley. He turned the corner, top hat all askew, carefully manicured orange beard and ragged accordion under one arm, metal triangle around his wrist, heavy instrument case of unknown origin clipping his leg or the brick road every third step. He saw me and set up shop, unpacking and squeezing out a song in record time, tapping the triangle like Pavlov's dipshit between the compression of his fingers on that tuneless monstrosity, and suddenly I was convinced he'd switched to this accordion because something unspeakable had happened to his guitar.

I was on him in seconds, standing him up by scruff of his collar, sneering in the fog of his coffee breath.

"Were you here this morning?"

He smiled and croaked a mournful note from the harmonic rig around his neck, and it was almost enough for me to snap right there. But I kept it together. Then I remembered the triangle.

The man has a triangle.

I buried my fist in his teeth, then kneed him in the bread box, then one more in the squeeze box, java breath burping from his gut and covering us in its toxic cloud. I put the toe of my boot through the teeth of the accordion's grill, and both of them made the same tortured squawk, and they both kept smiling. I'd never worn boots in my life until we moved down south, but after six months or so, Angie and I both ended up with a half dozen pairs each. Boots were assigned at birth in Kentucky, even if it meant you slipped on the sidewalks when they were wet. But one benefit was made clear when I booted my first adversary with those sharp leather toes. The term "shitkicker" made a whole lot more sense now, and a boot in the teeth was even more effective than a boot in the ass as far as changing a street musician's mind about smiling. That's when I was swarmed by a bevy of stinky street maestros avenging their friend. I would have thought it was just one busker zipping all around me in a tornado of weed and onions, invisible if not for the colorful tinkling of the holiday baubles in their beards. But fashionable beard bling made for great targets, and my fists were finding them easy.

So much for never punching anyone in Kentucky. It was a good run.

They seemed to be multiplying around me. A whole goddamn band now, including jug and spoon sections, and I beetled up on the street for protection, worried the alley would hide our brawl long enough for me to get hurt pretty severely by these dudes. However, I was soaking up any shots to my face like they were barely there, their fists and hard-earned guitar-string calluses rebounding off my skull like balloon animals. I wrote this off as adrenaline, or maybe their vegetarian diets, but I was still nervous enough to reach into my jacket for my secret weapon.

More like secret *weapons.*

My hand went deep into my pocket, then past that pocket, where the lining had torn, and my fingers found the extra pouch sewn into the back of the coat. The pouch was for hauling waterfowl, as my favorite winter coat was one of those rough but roomy hunting jackets you'd find at Cabela's, a seasonal sale near the lifetime table reservation they maintained for Ted Nugent. Angie got it as a gift back when she still harbored dreams of me bonding with her dad over hunting someday. Her dad was one of those guys who practically lived at Cabela's, even before the Nuge celebrity sightings, and he had killed every animal that made the mistake of wandering onto his property, always trying to goad me into going out and "getting us some ducks." But I'd had my fill of adventure with him early on, after I stayed at their cabin for Christmas and her dad went out for groceries and hit a deer with his car. He ran inside asking someone for help, and Angie said, "Go with him! Bonding!" and I threw on my duck jacket and climbed in his car. Her dad asked me, "Do they sell men's clothes where you got that?" and together we rode back to the scene of his crime. Once there, my job was to aim the headlights into the ditch while he bumbled around the dark with the .22 he'd pulled from a haphazard pile of pistols in the glove box. Somewhere past the ditch, I heard a gunshot, then a "Shit!" then another shot, and finally a panicked "Pop the trunk!" He emerged back into the light, blood streaked all over his chest, dragging this limp, gangly thing by its hooves and a lolling snout. Her dad was a hairy motherfucker, seemingly hairier than the deer, and there were several times I'd seen him from a distance and thought, "Isn't it too cold to be sleeveless?" and then he'd turn out to be shirtless instead. This night was no exception. I jumped out and ran behind the car and did what I was told, and there in the trunk was a coyote so frozen you could pick it up by the tail. He'd forgotten about the last thing he shot or hit with his car, so he was staring at it just as confused as I was.

Anyway! That was Greg, my new father-in-law, always asking if I wanted to kill shit with him, needling me to take a road trip back to his hometown of Lovelock, Mississippi, someday soon to go blast the souls out of some marginally dangerous beasts. I wanted to explain, "I don't want to kill ducks, New Dad," because up until five years ago, I was still brooding over the pet duck I had in third grade. Shit, you thought having pet ants were bad? I couldn't even *feed* the ducks with Angie in Cherokee Park near our house, let alone blow their heads off for sport. But I did accept the expensive hunting coat from Angie regardless, pretending I might hit the woods with her dad one day after all.

Because there was a silver lining to all this. Literally.

See, Greg was always giving me weapons, and this pleased Angie and her mom, who suspected Greg was probably undiagnosed bipolar, or at the least a little unhinged, and maybe I could be the son he'd lost. One time, Angie told me he'd put a bullet in their water heater because it "looked at him wrong." The icebox, too. She said he spent the good part of an afternoon explaining there were "eyes on everything," especially "if there was water nearby," whatever the hell that meant. But Greg ran out of room at his cabin for weapons, or shooting appliances, so he started slipping things to me. And among these knickknacks and hand-me-downs was all sorts of fun stuff: a straight razor, an old-timey police blackjack, even a tin badge that identified me as "Indian Police," which I guess let him hunt throughout Minnesota casinos with impunity.

But I had my own toys in that secret duck pocket, too. And this day being a very special occasion, I went for my "wedding present" instead, meaning the brass knuckles. Well, more accurately, they were presents for my groomsmen that I ended up keeping because I knew they wouldn't be allowed on their flights home. My brother had told them to put a little sticker on the knuckles that said "five bucks," so if they got flagged by the TSA they could claim they picked them up at a garage sale earlier that day. He also scratched the word "paperweight" across the bottom with his car keys. He said these same tricks worked when flying with handguns. We had our doubts.

So, since I was hesitating on whipping out the blackjack due to its legality in Kentucky rumbles, I decided on the polished fists I'd procured for my bestest men, which were 100% illegal. But I figured if you could commit a crime against humanity like playing an accordion in public, there was no reason they could outlaw such a wonderful, natural extension of a man's hand. Sure, the brass knuckles were originally jokes, but I quickly realized there was a whole subculture of knuckles mania online, all custom made, all very serious. And once I secured some beautiful knuckles for my brother Lloyd, I couldn't just give everybody else the chickenshit tin versions. So everybody got heavy-duty knucks, forged from nautical brass and surrounded by all manner of disclaimers and warning stickers. But Lloyd's still cost twice as much as the rest. This was because, growing up, he was the first person I'd ever seen in a real fight. And on that day, he was smart enough to put in his plastic football mouthpiece before he ran into the mob, which was the next best thing to wearing a huge rubber horse's head in a brawl. So he was smart enough to hide the Cadillac of Brass Knuckles from me whenever I came over looking to steal them back and complete my wedding collection, making me more of an "Indian Giver" than Indian Police, of course, despite my new badge.

Angie, she didn't mind the illegal weapon stash, as long as they were lined up on the curio cabinet instead, tucked alongside the Magic 8-Balls,

Civil War straight razors and mustache combs, headless sock monkeys, and my prized handful of fake snow from the *Dark Knight Rises* shoot in Pittsburgh. All that stuff didn't fit in the duck pocket. Believe me, I tried. But when we were packing up our huge apartment back in Steeltown, trying to figure out how to cram all that shit into our smaller place in Louisville, I did use the mini-arsenal as measuring tools, and my unlawful weapon collection transformed yet another depressing relocation and subsequent Tetris challenge into a much more entertaining game of Clue.

"Hey, Dave, how big is that picture frame?"

"Three straight razors and a sideways blackjack!"

"You realize there's a measuring tape right next to you, right?"

"Shhh . . ."

I hope by now it's obvious there was all sorts of stuff hidden in the lining of my coat, waiting for just the right excuse. Also, Angie was a big fan of *The Iliad*, particularly when the narrative would stop for no good reason just to tell you the history of the stick that someone's getting brained with. So apologies in advance of future beatings, but this is a motherfucking love story.

Back at the fight, there really wasn't much else to it. This was because, during the Apocalyptic Busker Beatdown, I'd circled back to the blackjack after all. What a twist! Always the blackjack, though. It felt like home. It might not have been as cinematic as a golden fist, but it sure as hell sent people to slumberland. A few cracks across the temple and half the musicians were on the ground dreaming of album covers they'd never autograph, while the other half were running for their lives, long, thin beards trailing like silk scarves. It seemed like some of them were trying some old-school WWF moves on me during the battle, but maybe that was my imagination. Do buskers dig wrestling, too? They did have that sort of earnest sincerity that suggested they'd totally believe in anything. But even to a bunch of gullible one-man bands, there is one big clue wrestling is fake (and you have to have been in an actual fight to realize it):

When things end up on the ground in real life, they stay there for good.

Still, I tried some moves, some kicks, just for kicks, some stuff from when I was a kid, or probably just picked up watching the half-ass efforts of the Keystone Wrestling League. Angie would have loved it. Cross chop, forehand chop, Mongolian chop. Wrestlers were always using those open-fist hacks instead of punches to minimize actual damage, but all that changes when you're chopping down trees with a blackjack. In fact, if you handed every professional wrestler a blackjack instead of a feather boa, the sport would finally be more respected than *Rollerball*, or at least roller derby. Do they still have roller derby? Does it still use horses?

Oh, yeah, there were some "clotheslines." Now *that* was a great visual punchline on the television screen. Facedown on the street, though? With nowhere to fly off your extended arm? It breaks bones. But one move I definitely landed was the Bronco Buster, since it fit the theme. It's where you ride a dude like a horse. Only I was the horse. Another twist! There was probably a Mule Kick in there, too, but that's as close as I ever came to a signature move. I guess a blackjack counts as a trademark match ender, but, honestly, "Go to Sleep!" will always be universal, no matter the tool, and certainly not relegated to an arena.

It seems like a no-brainer, but the one thing I did *not* do was break a guitar over anyone's head. Remember the ol' "El Kabong!" shout made famous by the cartoon horse Quick Draw McGraw? More specifically his vigilante alter ego and his patented guitar smash over all the bad guys' domes? I just couldn't do it. Guitars were now holy vessels.

After the bulk of the battle was done, I got up and blew some blood out my nostril, then crouched over Orange Accordion Man where he laid rigid. I grabbed him by his billy goat and gave him the open-palm "dicksmack" interrogation until he told me every corner where Louisville guitar players danced for their dinners. I wasn't even sure why I needed that info, because I'd driven by with the intention of leaving, not accosting the first singer-songwriter I saw. But suddenly I had this fantasy about being the seedy, sweaty fuck of a private eye right out of the movies, stumble-bumbling my way around Kentucky, beating the treble clefs out of hippies and hipsters alike. Then I remembered who I was sitting on again, and we played a little more blackjack with me as the dealer.

Whack whack whack, and another card for you, and another card for you, sir . . .

Afterwards, I returned to the guitar-shaped spot on the street. It was a huge mistake what I did next, but on the list of incriminating things I'd done since I'd received the news of Angie's death, it was barely in the top five.

I took out a piece of chalk and traced her from memory, drawing the crime scene I needed it to be. I outlined a guitar that wasn't there, and then the shape of my wife within it, just to see if she'd fit. Me, I fit inside easily this rendering. Even while standing. Even while walking. These lines were now my prison walls. I did this fast.

Quick Draw McGraw . . .

I guess I hoped this would help the police, too. Maybe one of the buskers was mad Angie didn't throw 'em a quarter? Or maybe she threw the quarter too hard. Or maybe our heated discussions outside Keep Louisville Weird about class theory and padlocks and cursed childhood ant farms drowned out all their terrible music and they'd had enough.

Then I saw Orange Accordion Man wasn't getting up, and the accordion wasn't smiling, and I worried they both might have stopped breathing for good. So I ran across the street to the Smoothie King and asked for some ice, remembering how Angie had done this weeks earlier when she went jogging too far and almost stroked out, calling me from the shade of a trash can, scared her body had stopped sweating. That was the most terrified I'd ever been. Until this morning.

I came back with the ice and poured some down the guy's shirt to see if he'd jump. Nothing. So I worked on the outline of the guitar some more, to make it perfect. I finished drawing us inside of it, then I collapsed on the sidewalk and put my arm around all three of us. I still wasn't entirely convinced my wife could fit inside a guitar case, let alone a guitar. But now everything seemed possible. And it felt like justice had sort of been served.

I might have blacked out.

***

I came to my senses and rolled toward the prone tunesmith, his shirt wet from the melted ice, my survival instincts kicking in. I was no doctor, by any stretch of the definition, and I couldn't even claim the rhetoric-and-composition PhD loophole, but my earlier ice-down-the-shirt diagnosis was good enough for me, and I got out my throwback '90s clamshell phone and called the police. I told them to check out some sidewalk art in the alley. Said it might help with their case, knowing full well it wouldn't. This, combined with skipping town before dusk on the same day I was informed of my new widower status, probably shot me right to the top of their most-wanted list. I imagined the head detective from my doorstep at that exact moment, taking my picture from the pile and pinning it to the tiptop of their pyramid of suspects, then, as an afterthought, grabbing a magic marker and adding a horse's bridle to my face.

I imagined the picture they'd choose was either my shittiest driver's license photo (good luck!) or my caller I.D. image on Angie's phone, which was no doubt in an evidence locker by now. On her phone, I would forever be wearing the leering rubber horse head from Keep Louisville Weird, which would be how Angie and the police would always remember me. Because no way a mugshot like that ever gets demoted from the top of *The $20,000 Pyramid* in a cop's bullpen, even if I did manage to catch the real killer.

But if you need closure on this particular day, if not this incident, later I would read in a true-crime adaptation of this case that the cops did search that alley "real good." But instead of pondering the important revelations of my chalk outline, they simply found a street musician in a coma, triangle somehow locked around his neck in a permanent chokehold, and an accordion that would need braces to ever sing again.

They would also find the rubber horse head I was wearing throughout the assault, though I'd swear on a stack of telephone books I had no recollection of ever buying such a ridiculous thing, let alone sliding it over my face when I stepped out of my car. But if I closed my eyes, I could clearly visualize the black-and-white snapshot of my grinning horse head in the middle of that dog-eared paperback, right where they always tucked in exactly eight pages of "shocking" photos. An artist's rendering would follow, the double-splash sketch of my horse head askew on my shoulders, golden fist clenched tight, hunting collar up high. I would vow to find a horse's head that fit a little better than that one, with maybe a smile that didn't look quite so crazy, but I'd never bother doing this.

But the novelizations were yet to come. As I left Louisville behind me that day, all I knew unequivocally was that my wife was dead. And I was probably going to jail. But, as I would find out, this would be a completely different sorta prison. One that nobody had ever seen before, even the inmates.

CPSIA information can be obtained
at www.ICGtesting.com
Printed in the USA
LVHW031244160821
695404LV00017B/2076

9 781943 720613